THOR'S FIERY MATE

GODS AND MONSTERS FATED MATES

BOOK ONE

REBEKAH R GANIERE

Thor's Fiery Mate © 2021 Rebekah R. Ganiere

ISBN: 978-1-63300-096-4
ISBN: 978-1-63300-097-1

Cover art by VWZDesigns

DEDICATION

For all the Book Wyrms out there.

NEWSLETTER

To claim your Two FREE Books and find out more about Rebekah R. Ganiere and her other Upcoming Releases
You can Go Here:
www.RebekahGaniere.com/Newsletter

All things pertaining to the Norse God, as well as Norse Mythology, are spelled in the Norse or Olde Norse way. You may notice a few words spelled differently in this series to align with the worldbuilding of the series.

- ***Hel*** - Daughter of Loki, but also ruler of Helheim. Therefore, in this series, hell is known as hel.
- ***Helborn*** - Those created by Hel to serve her.
- ***Helmarked*** - Those who have died and now reside in Helheim.
- ***Jötunn*** - A mythical Norse creature often known for being an ice or fire giant or troll. Used as a derogatory term.
- ***Yggdrasil*** — The World Tree connecting the Nine Realms. It is now the gateway that pulls all different realms together since Ragnarok shattered the Bifrost and caused rifts across the realms.

The Æsir (the main warrior-tribe of gods, who lived in Asgard)

• **Odin (Óðinn)** — Allfather; god of wisdom, war, death, and divine frenzy. King of the gods.

• **Frigg** — goddess of marriage, motherhood, the household, and prophecy. Queen of Asgard.

• **Thor (Þórr)** — god of thunder, lightning, storms, strength, and the protection of mankind. Wields Mjölnir.

• **Tyr (Týr)** — god of war, justice, law, oaths. Lost his hand binding Fenrir.

• **Baldur (Baldr)** — god of light, beauty, joy, purity, and innocence. The most beloved of the gods.

• **Hödr (Höðr)** — Baldr's blind brother; associated with winter and darkness. Tricked into killing Baldr by Loki.

• **Heimdall (Heimdallr)** — watchman of the gods; guardian of the Bifröst. God of foresight, vigilance, and beginnings. • **Vidarr (Víðarr)** — god of vengeance, silence.

• **Vali (Váli)** — god of vengeance; born specifically to avenge Baldr by killing Höðr.

• **Hermódr (Hermóðr)** — messenger of the gods; rode to Helheim to try to ransom Baldr.

• **Loki** — the trickster god, shape-shifter, sky-traveler, and mischief-maker. Of giant blood but counted among the Æsir.

• **Freyr** — god of fertility, prosperity, sunshine, peace.

• **Freya (Freyja)** — goddess of love, beauty, sex, fertility, gold, seiðr (magic).

Loki's children:

• **Hel** — goddess of death; rules the realm of Hel.

• **Fenrir** — monstrous wolf, prophesied to kill Odin at Ragnarök.

• **Jörmungandr (the Midgard Serpent)** — sea-serpent that encircles the world.

• **Sleipnir** — Odin's eight-legged horse son (born when Loki shape-shifted into a mare)

Other Norse Immortals:

• **The Norns (Urðr, Verðandi, Skuld)** — three fate-weavers who tend the well at the roots of Yggdrasil.

• **The Valkyries** — Odin's army and those who carry fallen warriors to Valhalla.

- **The Einherjar** — slain warriors who feast and train in Valhalla until Ragnarök.

CHAPTER ONE

Sutrelle sat, as tense as a drawn bowstring, under the weight of Thadren's massive hand on her thigh. She stared at her untouched plate, attempting to maintain control over the trembling threatening to consume her.

"Not hungry?" Thadren inquired, his deep voice like distant thunder rumbling through her body.

Summoning resolve, Sutrelle forced down a swallow, thinking only of sandpaper against parched wood. "Just overwhelmed by all this," she replied with a thin smile that didn't reach her eyes. Her gaze remained fixed on her meal- anything not to meet those fiery eyes of his.

His grip sent a sharp jolt down her spine, and she bit hard against the instinctive cry of protest rising within. Around them, the hall was alive with raucous laughter and boisterous singing- sounds mingling into a cacophony of revelry reminiscent of fevered creatures in the wild.

Her father's grand hall burned with smoke and heat, suffocating her. A giant blackened fireplace taking up much of one wall sported an entire mulboar roasting on a spit, its skin crackling and blackening with every revolution mimicking the death radiating inside her.

Every inch of open wall space in the room held trophies from her father's conquests, coloring the ashy colored walls with vibrance and variation to the otherwise drab room.

A nightloo from one world spread its wings wide, its mouth open, ready to strike. A fawndle from another world curled small, terrified, and cowering. A slipendot from a third world took up a massive space, its foot long fangs bared in a snarl. All decorations. Things to eliminate and display to show her father's power. Just like her betrothal to Thadren. All meant to show and garner loyalty and strength to his kingdom.

"Wait for our wedding night," Thadren breathed close enough for warmth to brush against her skin like embers from flame-hammered metal. "You'll never want to leave our bed when I show you true excitement." The prickle of his rust-colored beard brushed against her cheekbone. To Sutrelle's own disbelief, the scent he wore- a mixture of polished steel and exotic spices added a layer of intrigue amidst the anxiety swirling in her chest.

Surtr, Sutrelle's father, chuckled on the other side of Thadren and clapped the fire giant on the back with a massive, black hand. "I never thought having a daughter like Sutrelle would bring me anything but misery. It's good to know she will be of use to you and bring you some happiness, my friend."

Sutrelle's cheeks flushed at her father's jab. For as long as she remembered, she'd been nothing more than a burden and disappointment to her father, king of the fire giants. She wondered for the millionth time why he'd bothered to let her live after her mother died in childbirth. He'd always blamed her for the death of her mother, especially since her mother hadn't borne him any sons before bothering to die, as he constantly reminded her.

To look at them, you'd not know Sutrelle and Surtr were related. Where his eyes and beard glowed with fiery flames, her eyes were green. And though she'd been blessed with flaming red hair, it neither glowed nor burned like her father's. Not to mention his ten-foot-tall, ashen-skinned bulk towered over her diminutive frame. Nothing about Sutrelle said she was the daughter of a giant.

"Here, my dear." Thadren lifted a piece of goat from his plate, his massive hand engulfing it and making it look more like mouse kibble than an entire mouthful of meat.

Though he wasn't quite as tall as her father, Thadren had at least fifty pounds of muscle on him.

Thadren held the meat toward her lips, and the scent of it made her stomach growl and roil. The lingering smell of smoke and herbs mixed with the oily scent of the meat, and she swallowed back the bile that rose in her throat.

"You are as tiny as this bird," said Thadren. "You need to put some meat on yourself if you are going to bear our children."

"Ch-children?" she stammered. They weren't even married, and already he wanted her to give him children.

Thadren laughed. "Of course. With your beauty and my physique, our children will be the envy of the nine realms. We will be able to form alliances with other realms for the first time in generations." His hand left her thigh for the first time, and he stroked her cheek. "This marriage will allow me to avenge the wrongs done to my people, finally. With heirs to help rule, and your father's armies at my back, the only thing sweeter than the victories I achieve will be having you to warm my bed."

Sutrelle's nails dug deep into her knees as Thadren rubbed the meat across her bottom lip. Sutrelle opened her mouth and took the smallest bite possible.

Swallow it. Just swallow it.

Thadren chuckled and shoved the rest of the food in his mouth before sucking on his thick calloused fingers. "We will have to work on your appetite."

Sutrelle caught her father's seething glare over Thadren's shoulder. Her cheek no longer stung from where her father had struck her the week before, after hearing her pleas not to make her marry Thadren. But just because it no longer stung physically didn't mean the threat he'd made to her if she didn't marry Thadren didn't loom over her like a noose awaiting her throat.

Sutrelle cast her eyes downward.

"Forget about her. After tomorrow, you will have the rest of your life to do with her as you please. For now, we need to talk. I need to plan for my armies and what I gain out of the deal," said Surtr.

Thadren nodded, and Surtr stood as did everyone at the banquet.

Sutrelle got to her feet as her father turned without a word and headed for the exit.

Thadren looked to her and opened his mouth to speak, but the sharp bite of her father's call had him bowing to her and following his father like an obedient guard dog.

Sutrelle watched the men leave and stood before all her father's men, their eyes upon her. Some with pity, some with lust, and others with disdain. She lifted her thumb to her mouth and began to bite the skin next to her nail.

"Sutrelle."

She shoved her hands down and turned to the only friendly face she had known her entire life. Valkyrie.

The displaced Valkyrie had been like a sister to Sutrelle's mother. And after Ragnarök, when Surtr had kidnapped Sutrelle's mother, Valkyrie had insisted he take her too, though she would be a prisoner. But over time, Surtr had come to find Valkyrie useful and had tasked her with babysitting Sutrelle.

Valkyrie squeezed Sutrelle's arm, sending a jolt through her. Sutrelle straightened and lifted her eyes the way Valkyrie taught her.

"We should go," said Valkyrie.

Sutrelle nodded, and Valkyrie's hand dropped away as she squared her shoulders and turned to leave.

Sutrelle held her head high as she passed servants, Thadren's men, as well as her father's. She would never dare to assume such a posture if her father remained in the room, but Valkyrie told her if she ever wanted to garner an ounce of respect, she needed to at least try to appear like she possessed a shred of dignity. Easy for Valkyrie to say, she was a Valkyrie. Sutrelle was the unwanted daughter of a tyrant who took every opportunity to remind her how little she was worth.

They made their way to the farthest end of her father's palace. The corridor opened into a chamber carved from black volcanic stone, smaller than most palace closets. Rough-hewn walls softened by years of neglect. A narrow stone bed sat pushed against the far wall, draped in a single blanket dyed the color of dried blood, the only fabric Muspelheim's markets carried. A makeshift workbench dominated the opposite corner, its surface scarred with burn marks and littered with half-finished rings, pliers, and stones she'd polished by hand until her fingers bled. No windows, there were no windows this deep in the palace, but she'd mounted a row of tallow candles along a stone shelf, their stubs melted into pale pools that gave the room its only glow. The ceiling hung low, though for Sutrelle's slight frame it posed no problem. The bare obsidian floor was worn smooth under her feet from years of pacing.

She stepped inside, allowing herself to be cocooned by her space's familiarity.

She caught her reflection in the polished copper disc mounted beside her workbench- a makeshift mirror she'd hammered flat years ago. The face staring back was too delicate for the realm, all wrong for a fire giant's daughter. Her jade-green eyes, her mother's eyes, sat wide-set above fine-boned cheeks rather than being broad and heavy. Her thick auburn-ginger hair spilled in heavy waves past her shoulders, nearly to her waist, the copper tones catching the candlelight so that the strands themselves seemed to burn. The rough-spun tunic hung shapeless on her narrow frame, ash-gray and scratchy against her pale skin, which carried none of the molten undertones of her father's people. She looked away from the disc. She always looked away. At least if she didn't look at her reflection, she could pretend she looked like everyone else in the kingdom, except for the size. She barely came up to most males' chests.

The smell of her soap and candle wax, along with the metallic scent of her metalworks, soothed her. Brought her back to the present. To her safe space.

The sulfur stench from the corridor couldn't reach her here. The room, tucked behind two turns and a heavy door of riveted iron, that she shut behind her. Instead, she breathed in tallow smoke, the bite of heated metal, and the faded scent of the tallow soap cake Valkyrie had smuggled in, now whittled down to a sliver on the shelf. Beneath it all, the deep mineral tang of polished rocks and metal, cooling on her workbench. She pressed her back against the closed door. Outside, somewhere in the palace, the volcanic vents groaned and hissed, a low rumble she felt through the soles of her bare feet, vibrating up through the floor. But in here, the sound muffled to a distant pulse, almost like a heartbeat. Almost safe.

Valkyrie stood near the doorway, arms folded across her chest, her golden hair crushed against the stone doorjamb. Valkyrie was tall, almost a full head and more above Sutrelle, with a lean, athletic build. Her storm-gray eyes swept the space the way they always did: checking corners, cataloguing items, measuring threats, searching for anything amiss. Old scars traced pale lines along her forearms where they emerged from the rolled sleeves of her long coat, a battered thing the color of wet clay that hung past her knees and concealed, at least three blades. The coat smelled of oiled leather and ash. Valkyrie's jaw set in the same hard mask she wore everywhere, though the tension in her shoulders eased a fraction once the door clanged shut behind them. She positioned herself between Sutrelle and the only entrance without seeming to think about it. A habit, drilled deep as bone.

When she was young, she'd loved the amount of space in her room, until she'd searched the castle to find that her room was one of the shabbiest. Even Valkyrie's room had been furnished nicer-and she was a prisoner. Not that Sutrelle cared; her room was her own space. No one else entered, but Valkyrie, and only two servants ever came to summon her if needed. Where some might see the lack of furniture as a slap in the face, Sutrelle took advantage of the space and used the vacant area to store her books and all her mother's things. Sutrelle wasn't sure her father was aware she'd taken her mother's remaining possessions and put them in her room, but he'd never asked about them either.

Sutrelle sat on her bed, staring at her collection. A shelf of small wooden carved figurines Valkyrie had made for her as a child. A small sewing kit she used to mend her clothing when damaged. And, favorite of all, several groupings of stones she spent years collecting and polishing. She stared at her hands and pulled from deep within her. They glowed red, then white-hot as her magic pulsed through her veins, awaiting her command. A command she rarely uttered.

"Do you think I'll be able to take my things when I leave with Thadren?"

Sutrelle's gut clenched.

"No," said Valkyrie without pretense. "Because you aren't leaving with Thadren." Valkyrie strode to Sutrelle's bed, pulled out a dragon's hide bag, and tossed it to Sutrelle.

"Did you hear something? Is father making us live here?" She tried not to let her fear ring through in her voice.

"I've arranged a way out for us."

Sutrelle stared at Valkyrie. "What?"

Valkyrie hurried to the closet. "Take only things you cannot live without. Nothing of little consequence, and nothing that can be used against you."

"I... I don't understand."

Valkyrie grabbed a pair of plain pants and a muddy brown shirt from the back of Sutrelle's closet. "Put these on."

Sutrelle stared at the clothes. "But, Valkyrie-"

Valkyrie grabbed Sutrelle by the arms. "No. I'm no longer Valkyrie. I am Val, and you are Elle. I've made arrangements for us. I'm getting you out of here."

Val? Elle? Were they changing their names? What good would that do?

"How?" Sutrelle asked.

Val's golden braid swung back and forth as she shook her head. "There's no time to explain. I secured us passage. There's a place we can go. You can have a life free of your father, Thadren, and everything else. A place where you can be someone different."

Sutrelle bit the skin of her thumb. "But..."

Val grabbed her arms and pinned them down. "I promised your mother I would take care of you. I promised to keep you safe. I can't do that once you are married. I've been working on this for close to a year. I didn't tell you because I wasn't sure it would come through, and I didn't want to get your hopes up. But it came through."

Sutrelle swallowed hard. She wanted to leave. Gods knew she did. She wanted to be free, but... fear gripped her. If her father ever found her, the punishment would most certainly be death.

She shook her head. "They'll find us."

"Here you will never be anything more than you are right now. A rag doll to be used and tossed about by monsters. But you are so much more. Isn't the risk of death worth the possibility of true freedom?"

Sutrelle glanced at her hand, feeling the power inside her again. The power no one knew about except Val. Her father's fire and her mother's magic. Combined. Val had sworn her never to use her power because the moment her father found out about it, she would be his slave to his destructive will forever. Forced to use her magic to harm and maim and conquer. Things that would break Elle in the end.

"Come on." Val shoved the clothes into Sutrelle's hands. "Put them on."

Sutrelle inspected the clothes. Freedom. No more beatings. No more fear. The opportunity to figure out what she wanted to do with her life instead of being told. Wasn't that worth the chance?

She stripped off her gown and surveyed her belongings, trying to decide which were most important.

Her things. But they weren't her things. Not really. Everything in her room had either been her mother's or something secreted away without anyone knowing.

Sutrelle walked to the trunk in the corner and opened the lid. Inside a locket called to her. She'd made it out of scraps of metal she'd found around the castle. Mostly cast-offs from broken weapons. It had been the one thing she'd used her fire magic to make, melting and shaping the metal with her hands, literally. She ran her fingertip over the intricate design etched into it.

She slipped the locket around her neck, glad she would finally be able to wear it daily instead of only inside her room. It warmed her chest where it sat between her breasts. Inside, a portrait of her mother, drawn by Val, gave her strength. She picked up a worn journal as well.

Her books were replaceable. Her clothing as well. Not that she figured she would need long, drab gowns where they were going. The only other things she wanted had been her mother's.

She grabbed the dragon's hide bag, walked to her shelf, and began putting her figurines and rocks inside.

"Hurry," Val urged. "We have a long trip ahead. And we need to make sure we arrive before anyone notices we're gone."

“Don’t worry,” said Sutrelle. “Within the hour, the orgy will begin, and we will be the last thing anyone thinks of. Even Thadren.”

CHAPTER TWO
THIRTY DAYS LATER

"I can't believe I let you talk me into this." Thor ran his fingers through his hair and slid on his boots before tying the laces.

"I think it's your mother you have to thank. I simply asked if you would go with me because I have someone I need to meet, and I don't want to be roped into conversations with anyone looking for free legal advice," Loki replied.

Thor threw him a daggered gaze. "You mean a meeting you happened to mention in my mother's presence, which happened to be on the same night as her monthly masquerade feast?"

Loki chuckled and straightened his shirt cuffs. "Wrong again, my boy. Your mother set up the meeting. It's not my fault you're so nosy you eavesdropped on the conversation and got tangled up in her little scheme to marry you off."

Thor growled and stood from the edge of his bed. He didn't need marrying off. He'd been there, and that hadn't worked out, so giving it another try was not in the cards as far as he was concerned. Not that that stopped Frigg. Ever since the destruction of the Bifrost during Ragnarök, rifts had formed all over the nine realms. Rifts they'd tried to fix by remaking the Bifrost. But Odin's magic wasn't as it had once been, and so instead of connecting Asgard to Midgard, the Bifrost had somehow connected to Yggdrasil, the great ash tree connecting all worlds. In doing so, it opened up pathways between realms that the Asgardians had never realized existed before. Mount Olympus, Helheim, heaven, Valhalla, and Fólkvangr, Sheol and Gan Eden, Swarga Loka, Jingtu, and the immortal realms, Jōdo, Duat. Whatever realm was believed in after death, it connected to Yggdrasil. And as they had all grown restless in their respective afterlives, immortals used the rifts to move from realm to realm. And as such, the Norse god had moved from Valhalla to a realm of their own in Helheim. A realm that they had created and reigned over with the permission of Hel, Queen of Helheim. Not that she had much choice. When Odin said something was happening, it happened.

And ever since the move, Frigg had tried to set Thor up with every human and sup- supernatural who came into her pub or attended her masquerades. Frigg may want to see him happy, but she had no idea what weighed his soul down, and he doubted bringing a female into the mix would make anything better.

Even so, he appeased his mother by agreeing to attend her masquerades about every six months. Not that anything ever happened. For decades, he'd watched regulars show up and leave. Seen newcomers pair off with someone never to return. But for him, it was all routine. He went. He drank. He spoke as little as possible, and he left. Tonight would be no different.

Loki set his hand on Thor's shoulder for a moment. "It won't be any different if you don't give it a chance."

Thor shrugged off Loki's touch. "I hate it when you do that. Reading minds is creepy."

Loki shrugged. "I wouldn't need to if you opened your mouth and spoke more. You used to be so talkative. Couldn't stop talking as I remember. Mostly about yourself. Your conquests, victories, virtues, anything about you. But now-"

"Now I know better." Thor grabbed his leather coat and threw it on.

"I was going to say, now you are boring."

"And what about you?" Thor questioned. "I don't see you rushing out to find someone."

Loki flashed him a winning smile. "I don't need to. My bed is constantly filled with whoever I find companionable for the night. No strings. No expectations. Just fun. The way I like it."

Thor walked to the edge of his loft and took the metal stairs down to the floor of his shop two at a time. Bikes lined the walls of the solid brick structure. In the middle of the shop, his current restoration lay in pieces. Every section of the bike meticulously laid out and labeled.

"No time for fiddling with that," said Loki. "I still don't know why you mess with those things when you can fly."

"What about you and your squashed, brightly colored cars? You can fly, why do you drive those things?"

"Touché." Loki inclined his head.

"Besides," said Thor. "I like taking them apart and rebuilding them the way I want them. Gives me something to focus on." He didn't say it gave him something to focus on, so he didn't think about his failure to stop Ragnarök and the death of all their people.

Thor walked to his workbench and lifted his ancient hammer. Mjölnir had begun to feel heavier in his hand in the past century.

He wasn't sure if it was because of the things he'd done, or the things he hadn't, but he didn't care. The Thor of legend was no more, and what remained of him was nothing but a scarred shell.

"My car is out front." Loki headed to the exit.

"I can make my own way there." Thor lifted his hammer to the sky and, as always, disappeared in a flash of light.

Thor slammed onto the lawn in front of Frigg's mansion, making several people jump. The mansion rose behind a giant stone fountain like a relic of old Asgard transplanted into the Underworld. Pale stone walls threaded with climbing ivy, tall arched windows framed in white oak, and a pitched slate roof that disappeared into the perpetual cool haze overhead. No sun in Helheim, never sun, just the ambient glow of Helheim's ethereal illumination bleeding through the sky like a moon trapped behind gauze. The air smelled of rose petals and champagne, obviously a scent Frigg had conjured for the occasion. Gold-and-rust-colored leaves from the row of birch trees lining the cobblestone drive drifted across the grass in lazy spirals, pushed by an unseen breeze.

The center of the lawn in front of her estate sported a fountain carved from veined gray marble, depicting two ravens mid-flight, water arcing from their open beaks into a wide basin tinged green with age. The blush-colored rose hedges flanking it were still heavy with late blooms, their fragrance thick enough to taste, sweet and overwhelming, cutting through the mineral coolness of Helheim's air. Somewhere beyond the hedges, the low murmur of conversation, the clink of glasses, and dance music floated toward him.

Amongst the bushes and the fountain, several of Frigg's cats played and chased each other while various people watched. A fat orange tabby batted at a fallen rose petal while a sleek black cat with a crooked tail stalked through the hedgerow, belly low to the ground. A third, gray, imperious, the eldest, sat on the fountain's rim and watched the proceedings with the disdain of a creature who had outlived empires. At least five more cats scattered across the lawn, weaving between the legs of guests who stood in loose clusters on the grass, holding drinks and picking at plates of food balanced on the stone garden benches. The distant trill of a bird echoed from somewhere in the birch trees, mixing with the splash of fountain water and the cats' occasional chirping at each other.

He stowed Mjölnir in his inner coat pocket and strode to the door. A bluish-skinned man with protruding tusks nodded and let Thor in without so much as a questioning glance. One of the perks of being an immortal god who had thousands of stories made up about him over the centuries meant no one questioned who he was or his purpose for being somewhere.

He entered through the open stained-glass double door, and his gut clenched at the sight of the crimson and petal colored explosion that had taken over his mother's home. Frigg's private quarters had been transformed into a florist's fever dream. Garlands of dried roses in dusty mauve and deep burgundy draped from the ceiling beams, their papery petals floating down to land silently against the floor.

Silk ribbons in shades of cream and gold coiled around every chair back and bannister, and the long dining tables disappeared beneath towers of wine glasses, food plates, and desserts. Someone had stoked the hearth until the air felt thick, almost humid. Yggdrasil-patterned wallpaper peeked between swags of tulle, pinned with rune-etched brooches that glinted with silver and diamond under the ethereal overhead lights. Immortals moved around talking and dancing, drinking and eating. A feast for the senses. A light, soothing scent he couldn't place tickled his nose and made him relax a fraction. Frigg's own magic conjured a scent for each individual being. All based on what the being needed to help them relax and prevent fights. Masked eyes turned his direction, but then turned away. Well, this was going to be fun.

He spotted Frigg floating between tables in the room, talking and laughing. She stopped and turned, spotting him. She excused herself and headed his way.

"Has it been six months already?" She handed him a golden mask that materialized out of the air.

"Mother." Thor stared at the mask and snorted.

“I think it fits you.”

He shook his head and affixed the mask to his face, not that it would do any good at hiding who he was.

"Let's hope this time you find what you are looking for."

"I'm never looking," he said. “You are.”

Frigg's smile didn't waver. "Then let's hope someone else finds what they are looking for in you."

Thor nodded and turned toward the bar, but paused. "Oh, I almost forgot, Loki is coming as well. He's running late."

Frigg rolled her eyes. "When is he not?"

Thor smiled and kissed Frigg's cheek. “You look well, mother.”

She touched his face. “I wish I could say the same of you, but-” She stopped and looked over his shoulder. She smiled.

“Mingle and talk to someone new tonight, all right? For me?”

Thor couldn't promise anything, but he would at least try. If for nothing more than to keep her from making him come back for another six months.

Elle stared across the beautiful, expansive grounds of the mansion, where people milled. "Are you sure this is where Lady Frigg said we were to meet Loki?"

Val glanced through the gold gates, then at the paper in her hand again, before showing it to Elle.

Lady Frigg's mansion was all the paper said, and it was pretty hard to miss her mansion in Helheim. Especially the giant golden plaque over the ornate metal gates, bearing the images of two enormous cats. This was definitely the place. But it didn't look like a place to have a business meeting.

"Come on," said Val. "Let's get this over with, and then we can go back to Midgard."

Elle nodded. Val led her across the green and past a large marble fountain to the enormous, open, intricate, colored-glass front doors. Greenery and vines snaked up the front of the building. Standing near the entrance, a wide-shouldered, cobalt blue-skinned male nodded at people as they entered. Compared to how everyone else was dressed, Elle felt quite inadequate. Colorful jeweled masks covered their faces, matching the opulent silk and satin clothing they were draped in.

She stepped tentatively up the cream marble steps toward the entrance, and the light scent of old books and tallow candles made her gut clench, bringing back memories of her room back on Muspelheim. She'd lived in that room for so many years, she'd had no idea about the world outside of it. And moving with Val to Midgard had been exceptionally eye-opening.

Suddenly, the scent morphed into vanilla and spices, chasing away the memories and calming her.

Elle blinked several times at the bright reds and pinks decorating the entrance hall. It appeared to Elle more like Frigg had decorated the place in advance of a mating ritual than a home.

A beautiful young woman glided over to them and smiled at Elle. "Hello. I'm Fulla. You must be new here."

"Yes," Val answered. "I'm Val. We have a meeting-"

Fulla smiled brighter. "Of course. Lady Frigg said you would be coming." She looked at Elle. "You must be Elle."

Val's eyebrows smashed together. "I don't understand. We were told to be here at 8:00."

Fulla nodded. "If you will put these on and follow me."

Val looked from Elle to Fulla. The expression on her face told Elle that Val had no intention of putting on the mask and sitting at a table.

Val opened her mouth to argue, but Elle stepped forward.

"Thank you, Fulla." Elle took the masks and handed Val the silver fox mask while she herself affixed a golden cat mask to her face. Elle grabbed Val's hand and followed Fulla toward the tables lining a red velvet curtain.

"This is strange," said Val. "Why do we need masks to talk to Loki?"

"Maybe it's a game? Or to protect our identities? He has a lot of clients. I'm sure we aren't the only ones he is helping. Maybe he is trying to help us not be recognized. I'll get us some food, and you have a drink." Elle threw Val a smile, trying to ease the tension.

Ever since they'd run from Muspelheim, Val had been more on edge than ever. Lady Frigg had taken them in and offered them shelter, and Loki finally had the mortal paperwork they needed to permanently change their identities. It surprised Elle how many different pieces of identification mortals needed to be able to live on Midgard-

Earth. Humans call it Earth, she reminded herself.

Being in Helheim even for a few minutes had been overwhelming to Elle at first, but Midgard was a thousand times more. The sights, smells, and noise of Los Angeles, California, were nothing like what she was used to in Muspelheim.

On Midgard, the air tasted nothing like the metallic sulfur she'd grown up with. Instead, it hit her in layers- grease from a food truck, exhaust from a bus groaning through intersections, and underneath it all, the salty, faint smell of the ocean mixed with a thousand miles of concrete and asphalt.

June in Los Angeles meant a white, hazy sky pressed down without color or definition, the kind of sky one would have thought unthinkable in Muspelheim, where the horizon always glowed molten orange behind curtains of ash. On Midgard, the haze sat, bleaching and drying out the tops of palm trees to pale silhouettes.

It was nothing like Muspelheim. And that, she reminded herself, was the entire point.

The biggest thing she'd fought to become accustomed to in her new life was the lack of physical pain when she did something that displeased someone. On the contrary, the smiles and thank-yous liberally aimed her way for bringing people food and drinks were also something she wasn't quite used to yet, though they were most welcome.

Elle waited until Val had been seated and then turned toward the endless buffet tables. She lifted a porcelain plate while the two women in front of her finished choosing food. One sported skin the color of emeralds and wings hanging from the nape of her neck down to the edge of her heels. The other was the opposite, with skin as pale as alabaster and tiny feathery wings delicate enough to carry nothing more than a butterfly.

The women hurried away, talking animatedly and sending a sense of longing through Elle. She'd hoped when she and Val entered their new life, Elle might make friends, but the opportunity had yet to present itself.

Elle stepped up to the table and scanned the food. Since leaving Muspelheim, her appetite had also improved. She'd filled out the clothes Val bought for her better than she had at home. So much had changed in such a short period of time, bringing Elle joy she'd never known.

Elle picked up a chicken leg, some orange-looking rolls, several pastries she didn't recognize, fruit, and several types of cheese and placed them all on her plate. She looked down and, for a second, guilt stabbed her for taking too much.

"Eat anything you like, Elle. It's what it's here for."

Elle turned to Lady Frigg.

She curtsied. "Lady Frigg, thank you so much for your hospitality."

Frigg clucked her tongue and lifted Elle. "Elle, how many times have I told you that you do not need to do that anymore?"

Elle's cheeks flushed with heat. "I'm sorry, Lady Frigg, I-"

"Frigg. I am merely Frigg now. And you have worked for me for a month. You are safe here. Relax." Frigg placed a warm hand on Elle's arm and smiled at her in a way that made Elle's chest constrict. It was the kind, gentle smile of a mother. One Elle had always imagined her own mother would give her if she had lived.

"Of course, Frigg. I'm sorry."

"Do not apologize. You've done nothing wrong."

Elle nodded.

Frigg pulled Elle close and kissed her forehead. "My darling child, I look forward to the day when you no longer cower in fear.

The day you realize your true potential. Come. Let me sit you at a table and have someone bring you some mead."

"Oh, thank you, but Val is already at a table."

Frigg nodded and linked arms with Elle. "I know, but as she is busy at the moment, why don't you wait until she is done before rejoining her?"

Elle wanted to object, but before she could answer, Frigg pulled out a chair for her and sat her at a table near Val and a dark-haired man wearing a lion mask.

"Stay right here. I'll find you a drink." Frigg patted her shoulder and walked toward the bar.

Elle popped a grape into her mouth and scanned the room. People mingled and chatted. Several sat alone at tables, waiting for something or someone.

Elle grabbed a peach slice and chewed it as she pressed down her black skirt, though it had not a single wrinkle.

The soothing sounds of music floated over to her, the melodies foreign and bright. All the music on Muspelheim had been crude, boisterous, and tinged with anger. This music was completely opposite. Slow and light with hints of playfulness. She inspected the small raised platform where a dozen people dressed in white and wearing gold masks played various instruments. Some with buttons, others with strings, and one that someone hit with fabric-looking mallets. The sounds worked in harmony, lulling her into a cocoon of safety.

"I was asked to bring you this." A large hand came into view, holding a mug of mead.

Elle jumped and looked up and up and up into the bright blue eyes, framed by a golden goat mask.

CHAPTER THREE

Elle's nerves coiled tighter with each step the man took towards her, almost springing her from her seat. Her hands trembled as she fixed her gaze on him- butterflies staging a rebellion in her stomach, making it hard for her to catch a full breath.

"My Lady," he said, his voice velvety and calming. "Your mead?"

She froze, unable to nod in response. He placed the mug on the table and took a step back, allowing his presence to recede enough for Elle to breathe again. The atmosphere between them thick as spiderwebs spun by the Fates themselves. He brushed aside an unruly curl obscuring his vivid aqua eyes, framed by long lashes, watching her with a fascinating intensity.

Heat pulsed in her veins, and her magic swirled in her gut, making her tense.

She couldn't place his subtle scent, which reminded Elle of mountain air after rain, crisp and invigorating. The earthy aroma of the honeyed mead wafted up, warm and inviting, teasing with promises of liquid courage.

Though she couldn't see his entire face, he was the most handsome being she'd ever seen. Tall and broad-shouldered but trim at the waist. Not like her father's men, who were built like giant rectangular blocks of concrete.

The faint pulsing thrummed inside her at the sight of him. Warm and alive. It stretched out, making her tingle all over.

"May I join you?" he asked, his voice rolling like thunder.

Elle found her wits and nodded.

The chair across from her pulled out and creaked under the weight of his heavy frame. His hand clunked against the tabletop as his various silver rings hit it.

She recognized one of the rings, and her gut clenched. Terror flooded over her like a bucket of ice. The urge to flee rooted inside Elle as her heart hammered. It couldn't be. This could not be happening, and yet it was. There was no mask in all the universes that could hide his identity. Ozone. That was his scent. Ozone and electricity, like a lightning storm. And his eyes… those bright blue eyes and blond hair… He could only be one person.

Thor Odinson- God of Thunder.

Lady Frigg and Loki had gotten her out of Muspelheim, but somehow seeing Thor, her father's immortal enemy, made her want to run back. Word had it he hated both fire and ice giants alike. That he would rather kill them than breathe the same air they did. But here she sat, a half fire giant, across from the one man who possibly hated her more than her father did.

Her magic rose in her veins, and she clenched her fists tight to keep it from unleashing. She'd only ever used it when training with Val, and her magic was unpredictable at best. Plus, she had no intention of disrespecting Lady Frigg or her home by setting it on fire.

They stared at each other in silence for a long moment before he asked, "Do you have a name?"

Her throat dried, and she couldn't make her lips move.

A slight smile creased the corner of Thor's lips. "Shy? That's new. Most women here can't wait to tell you everything about themselves. Is this your first time?"

Elle nodded, and again they spent a moment staring at each other. Dressed in a black leather coat and T-shirt, his face sported some blond scruff. His square jaw and intense eyes were a perfect balance of handsome and terrifying.

"You're aware the purpose of this masquerade is to talk with new people and get acquainted, right?"

Masquerade?

She shook her head.

His eyebrows creased. "You aren't here for the masquerade?"

She lifted her hand but put it back down and chewed her lip instead, unsure how to answer.

Thor nodded and chuckled. "Ahhhh… so you got tricked into coming as well? Okay, so here's the deal. You see all the beings here? They are here to look for a mate or a companion or something… someone."

What? It was a potential mating gathering? She scanned the room as terror swept over her. That's not why she'd come. She'd come to procure papers. Papers to help her blend in on Midgard. Not to find a male companion. Did Val know that's where they were? Why hadn't Lady Frigg said anything?

Thor peered over her shoulder. She followed his gaze to the

table where Val talked to a long-haired man wearing a horse mask. Loki.

Loki and Val seemed to be having an animated conversation. Maybe she found out where they were, too. Had Loki tricked them into coming for some reason?

"Hey." Thor reached across the table and squeezed her hand.

She pulled away instinctively, and he raised his palms in defense.

"I'm sorry. I shouldn't have done that." He watched her for a moment. "You look like this might not be your kind of party. If you don't want to be here, I'll be happy to see you home. My mother will understand the mix-up."

Elle looked over her shoulder again at Val and Loki and then back at Thor. What did she do? Should she go to Val? The papers were important, she didn't want to interrupt them, but…

"Look," said Thor. "If you don't want to have dozens of males come try to talk to you, you should let me take you home." He held out his hand. She didn't want to go with him, but when a man in an eagle mask with deep red skin and pitch-black eyes spotted her and smiled, she involuntarily gripped Thor's massive calloused hand.

A pulse of heat passed between them and rushed up her arm and down into her belly. He looked down at her hand in his and then into her eyes. Confusion played over his features.

Elle yanked her magic back inside her, but it wasn't her magic that had heated their hands.

Elle jumped from her seat and glanced at the man with the eagle mask again. Thor followed her gaze and pulled Elle into his side. The eagle man stopped and inclined his head to Thor before heading in a different direction.

Relief filled Elle, but then nervousness gripped her again as Thor pressed his palm into the small of her back and escorted her toward the exit. Thor stopped and handed his mask to Fulla. A smile crept across her face, and she winked at him.

Thor led Elle through the throng awaiting to be let into the party. Elle should stop him. Move out of his grasp, but all she could concentrate on was the warmth of their connected hands, pulsating through her body.

Thor didn't know why he needed to help the timid, beautiful creature, but he couldn't help himself. Seeing her sitting at the table like a newborn doe had made his chest clench. Soft eyes wide with trepidation. Beautiful, thick auburn and ginger waves cascading down her back like a cloak of modesty. Slender fingers clutched together and trembling. He had no idea how she had ended up at the masquerade, but he was sure of one thing- she didn't belong there. Especially not while wearing a short, tight black skirt and sleeveless cream blouse. Both showed too much for his liking and, again, not enough. Either way, the clothes didn't seem like something she would normally wear. He saw her more in something soft. Flowy and feminine, then in something so… Midgardian. She seemed more like an innocent beauty that should be lazing in a meadow of flowers in Valhalla, instead of in the ashy grayness of Helheim.

He'd thought for a second she was a mortal, but the moment he'd touched her hand, he'd felt the power she carried within. A mortal didn't carry power like that. Perhaps she was a witch like Frigg. She definitely wasn't a succubus. Fae perhaps? Though he hadn't seen her ears to be able to tell for sure.

He pushed his way through the exit, and as soon as they stepped out the door, she took a deep breath and leaned against the stair railing as if it was the only thing holding her on her feet.

Standing outside Frigg's home, shrouded in moonlight, he wondered what the hel he was doing. He'd not been a savior of damsels in distress in centuries. But somehow, he couldn't help but want to protect the fragile creature who stood next to him.

"Where can I take you? Where do you live?"

She glanced up. "I... I'm not sure how to get there." Her voice came out so softly he'd almost missed it.

"Are you new to Helheim? I've never seen you before."

"I... I've been here about a month but... not down here."

"You live in Midgard?"

She nodded.

He realized that though she clutched the railing with one hand, their other hands still connected. Power radiated from her fingertips like a warm pulse of energy. He wanted to ask her what she was, but didn't want to pry. The way she looked at him made him think that one wrong question or stern word, and she might crumple. His appearance wasn't at its best, he had to admit, but she looked at him like he was a void dragon about to swallow her whole.

"Do you want me to take you back to Midgard? Can you find your place from there?"

"If... we go through the Raven Weaver."

His eyebrows scrunched together. "Frigg's place?"

"I... work there."

It wasn't possible. He'd been a bouncer at Frigg's weekly almost since the beginning, and he'd never seen her.

"How long-"

"Get out of my way!" A blonde beauty with storm gray eyes and a deadly expression stomped out the front door. She pulled a long coat around her shoulders, spotted them, and strode toward them.

"Elle!" she scolded. "What are you doing out here? I told you to wait for me."

Elle? The beautiful creature's name was Elle.

Elle wrapped her arms around herself. "But... I was supposed to talk to different men. It was a mating party."

The woman retracted the blade at her wrist and stepped up to Elle, tore the mask from Elle's face, and tossed it to the ground, where it promptly disappeared. She pulled Elle from Thor and looked her over as if checking to see if Thor had hurt her.

"Hey," he protested. "I was helping her. Who are you?"

"Val," said Loki, jogging down the steps to join them.

Val glowered at Loki. "I am more than capable of answering and taking care of myself, thank you."

"So you've told me. Twice already." Loki smiled broadly.

Val rolled her eyes. "We should go." Val wrapped an arm around Elle's shoulders and propelled her down several steps.

"Wait." Thor reached for Elle's hand again but missed.

She turned, and he got a good look at her face for the first time. The sight made his gut clench. A smattering of delicate freckles scattered across her porcelain skin, like stars on a moonlit night. Her eyes, ensnared him with an intensity both all-consuming and unnerving. High cheekbones, sculpted as if by the chisel of a divine artisan. Her lips, full and lush, beckoned him to linger a moment longer.

As he stood before her, haunted by ghosts of a past too painful to relinquish, he found himself drawn to the enigma she presented. Each feature spoke of a sorrow masked by serenity. The air around them thickened with tension, a tangible cloak that draped over their shoulders. He fought for something more to make her stay, but he couldn't find words.

Val pulled on Elle's once more. "No waiting, Odinson. We are leaving."

Thor wanted to say something else, but had no idea what the relationship was between the two women; if it had been anything untoward, Loki wouldn't have stood by. Even he wasn't that bad.

Elle stared at him for a moment and dropped her gaze to the ground. "Thank you for your kindness, Thor Odinson."

The way she said his name shot him straight in the heart.

"When do you work next?" he asked without thinking.

Val scowled, took Elle by the hand, and propelled her forward.

Elle turned over her shoulder. "I work every day."

Val said something to her, and Elle continued across the lawn toward the outer gate and into the mists beyond.

Every day? Well then, maybe-

It was too late. They'd disappeared into the mist.

Thor stared at where they'd just stood. Who was Elle, and why did she need a caretaker? Why was she in Helheim? He rubbed his fingers together, remembering the strange warmth that had stirred within him at the touch of her soft, delicate hand.

Loki chuckled and slapped him on the shoulder. "Has the mighty Thor finally found a match?"

"Who is she?"

"The blonde?"

Thor growled, making Loki chuckle harder. "Easy. Her name is Elle."

"I got that. Elle who?"

Loki shrugged and looked away. "Just Elle."

Thor's gut told him Loki was lying. "Why was her friend talking to you?"

"You know I can't tell you that, privilege and all."

"That's stupid human B.S. You don't even believe in it."

Loki sighed. "They needed some papers to live on Midgard. Human stuff. I helped them out."

"Where are they from?"

Loki held up his hands. "If you want any more information, go ask her yourself. I'm not a messenger or information god. Herm is the one you want for that."

Thor eyed him. "You seemed in unusually banterous form with her blonde friend, Val. I thought you said you were happy with your rotating bed partners."

Loki gritted his teeth and focused on the direction the women had gone. "Val is business, nothing more."

Thor snorted. "I saw how you followed her out. How you looked at her."

"I was simply making sure she found her friend."

Thor snorted. "You keep telling yourself that, cousin."

Loki's eyes flashed icy, and for a minute, Thor thought he might say something more. Instead, he gave his ever-annoying smug smile, removed his suit jacket, and loosened his tie.

"Are you fighting tonight?" Thor asked.

"Yes." Loki removed his cufflinks and put them in his pants pocket. "I promised Baldur a rematch. Again."

Thor nodded. "Then I'll see you at the Throne."

Once, just once, he wished someone other than himself would hand Loki his pompous ass in the fight ring. But if he couldn't get that, maybe getting out some of his own pent-up energy in the ring would be as good.

He lifted Mjölnir and jumped.

CHAPTER FOUR

Val set three steins of beer on the tray in front of Elle, sitting on the polished honey-colored bar, and pointed to a table. "Take these to table one."

Elle stared at the portal down to Helheim.

“Elle!”

Her gaze snapped to Val, who pointed at the tray before turning to the shelf behind the bar and grabbing a bottle of rum.

Ever since meeting Thor the night before, she'd been able to think of nothing else. Elle lifted the tray and headed to one of the humans' tables. She set the mugs down and returned to the bar without realizing it.

None of the stories she'd heard her father tell about the horrible monster of a man who brought nothing but death and destruction to all who opposed him in the nine realms seemed to fit the gentle giant who had thought of nothing but her peace of mind. And when he'd touched her hand, something had sparked inside her.

Something she'd never felt before. A part of her she couldn't reach on her own, nor define. Not her magic. Something different. Something…

She rubbed her fingertips together, trying to recreate the warmth he had produced within her.

"Elle!" Val grabbed her shoulder.

Val pushed a stein toward her and jerked her chin toward the corner. "Get it together."

Elle's cheeks heated as she picked up the beer and headed toward the table. She didn't need anyone to tell her where it went or who it was for. The golden-eyed immortal who worked as a bouncer in Frigg's Raven Weaver topside pub was known to everyone in the nine realms.

She put on a smile and headed straight for the solemn, hulking figure.

"Hello, Heimdall." She slid the beer to him.

"Lady Elle. How are you today?"

No one had called her 'Lady' back when she'd been princess of the fire giants, so to hear someone on Midgard call her that seemed especially strange.

"It's Elle."

Heimdall took a long swig of his drink. "You and I both know that is not true."

Elle chuckled and rolled her eyes. Heimdall, as well as Lady Frigg, had treated her with nothing but the utmost respect since she'd arrived. In the past month, they'd made her more welcome than she ever had been back at her father's court. Even so, the idea that someone would recognize her still made her nervous- and calling her Lady was one small step closer to being possibly recognized.

Heimdall squeezed her hand and winked at her. "Don't worry, your secret is safe."

"What secret?" a deep voice rumbled behind her.

Elle turned at the sound, and her skin warmed as she pulled her hand from Heimdall's grip. Her gaze traveled from Thor's handsome, chiseled face to his fathomless eyes. Unlike the night before, he was clean-shaven, and the faint scent of soap and cologne wafted off him instead of ozone and electricity.

She shivered at the delicious mixture.

"Thor," said Heimdall, "I can't remember the last time you set foot in Midgard. Should I be afraid for my job?"

Thor moved around Elle, his body brushing up against hers and making a pulse of heat rush through her. He sat in the booth opposite Heimdall and stole a swig of beer.

"Buy your own." Heimdall pulled the stein back across the table.

A table down the row broke out into cheers and banging on the table for several minutes as they high-fived and gulped down all their drinks. She looked at the table, calculating how many more pints she would need to bring them, and then looked back at Thor.

"Would you like a beer?"

"Please, Elle."

She looked up at his use of her name. Her heartbeat quickened at his smile. She retreated to the bar, trying to slow her racing heart. He'd found her. She'd hoped he would, but the fact that he was really there brought up mixed emotions.

Val had given her almost an hour-long lecture when they'd gotten back from Frigg's the night before. All about what would happen if Thor found out her identity.

Elle chewed the skin around her nails as she waited for Val to finish filling other orders. Confusion swirled inside her. She'd never felt so… strange before. In Thor's presence, the tumultuous fusion of scorching heat and bone-chilling cold burned her. Despite being raised to conceal herself, to exist in the shadows without a voice, an indescribable force robbed her of speech whenever she crossed paths with Thor. Was it the dread of his discovering her as the offspring of his eternal adversary, or something far deeper? If he'd shown up a minute earlier, he would have heard Heimdall call her 'Lady', and then what would have happened? She wouldn't be able to hide from him forever, but the idea of him looking at her with rage and hatred made her gut twist. When that happened, would she even still be able to keep working for Frigg, or would he insist she be sent away? Or worse, would he tell her father where she was?

"What's wrong?" Val startled her, making her jump.

"Uh… nothing." Elle bit her thumb.

"Why are you flushed?"

"Am I?" Elle touched her cheek.

Val eyed her. "You're chewing your fingers again."

Elle dropped her hand. "I need another beer," Elle said, not meeting Val's probing gaze.

"Which table?"

"Heimdall."

Val's eyebrows slammed together. "He never drinks more than one an hour."

"It's not for him."

Val glanced at the table, and her eyes darkened. "Elle-"

"I didn't ask him to come."

"We've talked about this. If he finds out who you are-"

"Lady Frigg knows. And Heimdall and Loki-"

"But Frigg, Heimdall, and Loki didn't try to kill your father. And thousands of fire giants. And vow to kill them all after Ragnarök." She looked around. "And though most of these are mortals, any number of sups pass through here who, I am sure, would be more than happy to sell you out for money or favor with Surtr."

Elle's fists balled. "Then why did we run? Why did we come here if I'm still going to spend the rest of my immortal life looking over my shoulder? I might as well have stayed and let Thadren have his way with me. At least with him I would've been protected."

Val crushed a lemon in her fist. "You are protected. I will protect you. But I want you to be careful."

"And stay away from Odin's son?"

"Yes."

Val wouldn't be happy with anything but her agreement to stay away from Thor, but somehow, she wasn't sure that was a promise she could make.

"I'll do my best. But I can't ask him not to come to his mother's establishment. That would be more suspicious than if I do nothing."

"Then continue to do nothing. Don't be discourteous, but don't encourage him either. If Thor Odinson finds out who you are, you can bet he will want one of two things: to use you to hurt Surtr, or to kill you to hurt Surtr."

Elle snorted. "Too bad he doesn't realize my father would have killed me himself if he'd cared enough about me to lift a finger."

When Elle escaped with Val, she'd anticipated her life getting easier, not harder. She shook her head. She should have known better.

"Problem?" Frigg appeared next to Elle and smiled. "What can I do to help?"

"Tell me about her." Thor's gaze remained on Elle as she moved about the bar in her dark, tight leggings that hugged her slender hips in a beautiful temptation. Once again, he didn't like her wearing something so sensual around other people, but he had no idea why it bothered him.

"Who?"

Thor rolled his eyes. "Elle."

"Ahhhh..." Heimdall sipped his beer but didn't say anything.

"Ahhh? That's all you have to say? Ahhh?" Thor waited a moment. "Heimdall."

Heimdall shrugged his heavy shoulders. "Not much to tell. She got here about a month ago with her friend. They were looking for work. Frigg needed help and hired them."

"Where did they come from?"

Heimdall wouldn't meet Thor's eye.

Heimdall had never not told him something before. They'd always been honest with each other.

"Where are they staying?"

Heimdall rotated his stein. "I believe they are staying here."

"Here?"

"In the apartments upstairs."

"Hello, Odinson." Frigg set a beer in front of Thor.

He scanned for Elle and found her serving another table.

"Hello, mother." Thor picked up the beer and swigged it. Though she wasn't biologically his mother, Frigg had taken him in as a baby, treating him like one of her own, and had always raised him as such. Just like all the other children of Odin that hadn't been hers by birth.

She ran her fingers through his hair. "You're letting it grow again?"

He shrugged. "Not as long as it used to be."

She smiled. "I liked it long."

"Are you giving shelter to Elle and her friend Val?"

She planted a smile on her face and blinked innocently. "If you are asking if they are renting rooms from me and working for me, then yes."

Thor growled. "That's not what I mean."

Frigg patted him on the head. "Well, that's what I mean, son."

It was common knowledge within their family that Frigg had an open-door policy for helping those who wanted to relocate to Midgard or to their area of Helheim. It was how they'd all gotten there in the first place. Frigg had helped relocate hundreds of people over the years. But somehow this time it felt different.

Thor's gaze followed Elle from table to table.

"If you don't stop eyeing my help, I won't be able to find anyone to work here," Frigg teased.

"What can you tell me about her?"

Frigg chuckled. "Oh no. I'm done playing matchmaker for my children."

"Wasn't it you who made a point of nagging me to go to the masquerade last night? You know the party you throw every month, specifically to help people find love."

Frigg's mouth fell open in mock outrage. "Nag? I never nag, Thor. I simply suggest things. Multiple times if necessary."

Thor cocked an eyebrow at her.

"If you want to understand Elle, talk to her," said Frigg. “Maybe not while she is working, though. You make her unable to concentrate, and I don’t want all of my mugs broken by the end of the day.”

"I want to talk to her, but her friend doesn’t seem to like me too much."

Heimdall chuckled. “That must be new for you. A woman *not* liking you.”

Thor flipped off Heimdall, who laughed harder.

Frigg sighed. "Elle... has been through a lot. She's had a hard life. Val is just protective of her. If what you are looking for is some fun, please, Thor, for her sake, pick someone else. Anyone else."

Frigg’s words stung more than he wanted to admit. "How long has it been since you've seen me want to have fun with a woman?"

“Technically, I’ve never seen you have fun with a woman, thank gods. But… Since I’ve seen you look at a woman?” She patted his shoulder. "Too long."

"I don't want fun," Thor admitted. "I want..." What did he want? "I want to know her."

Frigg searched his face for a moment. "Then do it. But go slow. Elle is... fragile."

Thor glanced over at Elle again. Frigg's description of Elle seemed correct. But Thor remembered what he had felt when he touched her. Power. Deep, raw, untapped power.

"And be careful."

"I am not going to hurt her," Thor said.

"I didn't mean her. I meant you.”

What did that mean? What did Frigg see?

“But, if you want Elle, you have to go through Val." Frigg smiled. "And may the gods be with you on that front."

He waited for Frigg to move on to her other guests before turning back to Heimdall.

Heimdall studied him. "You like her."

"I don't know her."

Heimdall smiled. "What does that matter? You know better than anyone you cannot stop fate."

Thor gritted his teeth. Heimdall had been trying to help Thor release his guilt over Ragnarök for centuries. The problem was, it was the first battle Thor ever lost, and it ended with his home destroyed and all its remaining inhabitants displaced.

"Is that what she is? My fate? Both you and my mother see what lies in my cards, so tell me and save me some time. Is Elle my fate?"

A part of him wished more than anything that the fiery-haired beauty was his fate. The part that hadn't been able to do anything other than think of her all night and all morning. Even when he'd been in the ring fighting. Afterward, when he'd gotten drunk and fallen asleep in one of the guest rooms at his father's bar. And then first thing when he'd woken up and headed home to shower. That part of him had been able to do nothing more than remember her scent, her eyes, her soft smile. But another part told him that, after everything he'd done, he didn't deserve someone like Elle.

"I cannot tell you the future," Heimdall replied.

"Why? You've done it tons of times before," Thor countered.

"Yes, but…" Heimdall stared at him for a long moment, his golden glowing eyes glazing over.

Heimdall saw something. Something in the future. Thor had seen that look in Heimdall's eyes a million times before.

Finally, his eyes cleared and dimmed. "The things I've told you have involved the fate of the nine realms, not the fate of your love life."

Thor glared at Heimdall, trying to let the weight of his gaze push Heimdall into speaking, but it was pointless. Heimdall didn't bow to anyone but Odin- and he only did that out of respect. Heimdall was both older and more powerful than even Odin.

"So you won't tell me?"

Heimdall shrugged. "Wouldn't you rather be surprised by how it plays out than ruin the ending?"

"Not this time." For some reason, that was the truth. Thor didn't like knowing the end of the story before it started, but this time, something told him he needed to know.

Heimdall chuckled. "Well, too bad, old friend. I don't want to spoil how it ends before it gets going. If it were a book, I'd rip out the last chapter so neither of us peeked."

Thor growled and clenched his beer. Okay, so for some reason, no one would help him cheat this time. He had to do things like a mere mortal wanting to get to know a woman. The thought both intrigued and aggravated him.

Suddenly, an idea popped into his head.

"Fine. If you won't help, I'll find someone who will."

Heimdall shook his head. "You already asked him, and he wouldn't say anything. Are you sure you can trust what he tells you now?"

"Who said I am going to ask him to tell me something?" Thor pulled out his phone and pressed speed dial. The phone rang several times.

"Odinson, how interesting to hear from you twice in two days."

"I need your help," he said without pretense.

Silence filled the line for a moment.

"Well, well, well. I can't remember the last time the Mighty

Thor, son of Odin, needed my help. Oh, wait, yes, I can. It was when-"

Thor's hand clenched tighter around the stein. "Are you going to help me or not?"

Loki paused. "Of course, cousin. What do you need?"

“Meet me at Frigg's. Midgard side.”

"When?"

"Now."

CHAPTER FIVE

"Let me get this right," Loki said with a flourish. "You, Thor, God of Thunder, want me, Loki, God of Mischief, to distract a bartender so you can talk to a girl. This is why you called me all the way up here?"

"No, I called you up here because I want you to touch Elle and tell me all about her, and then tell me what you see the possibilities of the future to be. But you won't."

"Sorry," Loki said. "I made a promise."

Dammit. Why was everyone being so secretive all of a sudden? Usually, everyone was more than willing to help him with whatever he needed. With how much nagging he'd gotten over the last hundred years about not being alone, he would have thought everyone would be more than overjoyed to help him. Instead, it was almost like the opposite.

"Am I the only one you two won't help, or are there others as well?"

Loki shrugged. "I'm not one to gossip."

Thor snorted.

"Is our business concluded?" Loki looked at his watch.

"Oh, please, don't act like this was such an inconvenient trip for you. You had to do what? Focus on the pub for five seconds before you were able to transport here?"

"Do you have any idea what my time is worth? What I charge per hour?"

"Well, plan B won't take an hour. She gets her fifteen-minute break in less than five minutes," said Thor.

"After sitting here, it will have been half an hour, which equals-"

"One bottle of Odin's reserve ale? Done," said Thor.

Loki's eyes widened slightly. "Not so fast. I agree on the ale, but you will also owe me a favor."

"What favor?"

Loki's eyes twinkled in a way that reminded him of Frigg, and a smirk settled on his chiseled face. "I'll tell you when the time comes."

"That's not a deal I would agree to if I were you," said Heimdall.

"Better decide fast, Odinson," said Loki. "Your girl took off her apron and is headed for the stairs to the lofts."

Thor looked over his shoulder toward the staircase, which led to the upper-floor apartments. Elle had almost reached the bottom step.

"Looks like Val is not far behind," Loki prodded.

He was going to lose his shot. "Deal." Thor jumped from the table and headed for the stairs. He hit the bottom when he heard Loki's voice behind him.

"Well, Val, fancy meeting you here," Loki said loudly.

Thor didn't wait for a reply, but he got the feeling Loki would have helped Thor for a chance to talk to Val without ale or favor attached.

Taking the stairs two at a time, he reached the top as Elle put the key in the lock of one of the doors.

"Elle."

She jumped. "Th- Thor. Did... did you need something?" She pulled the key from the lock and backed up a step.

He slowed his pace and held up his hands. "I wanted to talk to you."

She scanned the hallway like a scared rabbit. "All right." She dropped her gaze and let her hair fall over her face.

He stopped in front of her, his boots scraping softly against the carpet. The sounds from the bar below barely hummed in the background. He wondered if Frigg had magicked the apartments so they weren't bothered by the sounds. His heart hammered, a wild and erratic rhythm, as though it had forgotten he'd ever spoken to a woman before. If anyone had asked him moments earlier, he would have claimed to be confident- charming even- but standing face-to-face with her, every practiced word he'd rehearsed over the last day evaporated like the morning mist.

Her hair, a cascade of beautiful fiery spirals, swayed with her movements. He couldn't help but notice how the golden undertones caught the light, shimmering like a flickering fire.

When he truly looked into her eyes without the obstruction of her mask- it was as if he'd stepped into an entirely new world. They weren't just green; they were flecked with tiny bursts of amber and gold that seemed to dance. She didn't look at him- she studied him, peeling back his layers with quiet curiosity. He'd never felt more exposed and yet oddly seen, as though she read every thought racing through his mind.

Close enough now, her scent reached him: a mix of freshly poured ale and something darker, smokier- a whisper of charred cedar lingered on her skin. It wasn't cloying or sweet like the perfumes other women wore; it was raw and earthy, grounding him as it stirred something primal deep within his chest. He swallowed hard against the sudden dryness in his throat and forced himself to speak.

"You're…" His voice cracked, betraying his nerves. He cleared his throat and tried again. "You're not what I expected."

"And what did you expect?" she asked, her voice smooth but laced with amusement.

"I-" He hesitated, raking a hand through his hair. The words heavy on his tongue, unrefined and inadequate. "I don't know. I mean… not this." He gestured toward her like a fool, then regretted it. "Not you."

Her eyebrows arched. "Not me?" she echoed, tilting her head to one side. A strand of hair fell across her cheek, and before he thought better of it, he reached out to brush it away.

His fingers froze an inch from her skin when he realized what he was doing. He let his hand drop back to his side, heat blooming across his face.

"I didn't mean it like that. I just… I didn't think…" He trailed off again, cursing himself.

"Would what?" she pressed.

"Would speak to me again," he admitted.

For a moment, she didn't respond. Her eyes searched his face. Her brilliant green eyes narrowed as though weighing his sincerity. "Why not?"

"After how your friend acted and spoke to me, I figured she managed to warn you off me."

"Warn me off?"

His gut clenched. He couldn't tell if she was really as innocent as she sounded, or if it was a ruse of some sort.

"Yes. You know, Thor Odinson, bedder of women. Eternal Playboy. Loner who never wants attachments."

Her eyes widened. "So, you sleep with lots of women?"

"Yes. I mean no. Well, yes, I used to centuries ago, but not in a long time." Why had he said that? What in the nine realms was wrong with him?

"But that's common knowledge about you?" she asked.

This was not the way he thought this conversation would go. Why was he talking about women he'd bedded? What was wrong with him?

She laughed. A low and melodic sound that sent a shiver down his spine. Not a laugh meant for show or politeness; it was genuine, warm in a way that made him want to hear it again to see if it would feel as good the second time.

"Well, I'm glad I am not your millionth conquest this decade."

"Have I conquered you then?" he teased.

Her smile widened- a real smile now- and for the first time since approaching her, some of the tension left his body. Maybe he wasn't hopeless after all.

"Sadly, it takes a lot more than getting me a mug of mead and helping me out of a house and down some steps for me to be conquered."

"A lot more?"

"Yes. After all, what kind of lady do you think I am?"

All he focused on was her. The way her presence filled every empty space around him as though she belonged there. The way her eyes invaded him while her words remained teasing.

A moment passed. Then another, and finally her cheeks burned a beautiful shade of rose.

"So," she said. "Are you going to keep staring at me? Or is there something you came here to say?"

He blinked, startled back to reality.

"I... I'm glad you made it back safe last night," he blurted.

What the hell was going on? That's not what he wanted to say.

"Thank you." She folded her hands in front of her and shivered.

"Are... are you cold?" Without thinking, he ran his hands up her bare arms, making them pebble.

Their gazes connected, and something inside him moved. A piece of him he'd buried away. One he'd sworn he'd never allow out again. A part of him he'd thought he'd lost under the years and years of fighting and killing and drinking. But somehow, the beautiful, timid creature brought that piece of him back from the brink of death.

She dropped her gaze to where his hands rested on her arms. "Why... does it feel like that when you touch me?"

"I don't know. Has it never happened to you before when someone touched you?"

She shook her head. "I've only ever been touched by two other people. Val and... someone else. And neither of them ever made my skin feel like embers were burning from underneath it."

Thor swiped his calloused thumb over her skin and waited for it to burst into flames.

"Where did you come from?" he asked.

"You're a god. And you have children of your own, so I'm told. I would think you'd know where babies come from."

He caught the tickle of a smile cross her lips again. "Is that a joke? Did you make a joke?"

She chuckled.

"You know what I mean. Where were you before you came here? Why did you decide to come to Midgard?"

She shrugged. "I'd never been. I wanted to see what it was like. Wanted to see what humans were like. I'd heard many tales of them throughout my life. I wanted to see for myself. Why did you move to Helheim?"

"Valhalla grew boring. I was restless. Centuries of fighting aren't erased because you go to paradise." He lifted a strand of her hair and rubbed it between his fingers.

"Why are you doing that?"

He peered into her bright eyes. "Do you want me to stop?"

Her eyebrows scrunched together. "I... I'm not sure."

ELLE'S HEAD SPUN AT HIS NEARNESS, MAKING HER UNABLE TO THINK straight. She'd never been touched so tenderly or intimately before. The way his eyes clouded with pain and something else she'd never seen intrigued her and made her want to hold him close and hug his bad memories away. But she played with proverbial fire. When he found out who she was-

Thor's breath hovered so close Elle almost tasted the heat of it on her skin. Her gaze flitted upward, colliding with his- intense with turbulent white lightning that threatened to sting her if she looked too hard. His fingers skimmed the air near her cheek, a ghostly caress that lingered, then retreated too fast.

He leaned in and smelled her hair. Her skin blossomed into an inferno, and she couldn't help the sigh that crawled up her throat.

What was happening with her? She'd never experienced feelings for a man before, not that she'd had much opportunity. The only men she ever saw were her father's men. Fire giants. Half giants. And any other thugs he'd managed to dominate. Not one of them looked at her with tenderness or kindness. And none would have dared to touch her for fear of having their hands removed. And their arms. And their-

"Are you okay?"

She blinked. "Yes. Sorry."

"I want to take you somewhere."

She should say no. She should excuse herself and go to her apartment for the rest of her break.

She did neither. "Where?"

His eyes widened as if surprised. "Anywhere you want. You tell me, and I'll take you there."

"I... I don't know anywhere to go."

"Then I'll decide."

"What will we do?"

"Anything we want. What do you like to eat?"

"Uh... the usual things. Food." She couldn't tell him what she normally ate without him figuring out where she came from.

He chuckled. "What about sushi? Have you ever eaten sushi?"

Her eyebrows creased. "Sushi?"

"It's raw fish."

She wrinkled her nose. That sounded terrible. Who would want to eat raw anything?

Thor smiled. Not in the way she was used to. Not a mocking smile, or a leering smile, just a genuine smile.

"Trust me, it tastes better than it sounds."

She peered at him. Was he jesting with her?

"How about tonight? We could-"

"Elle!"

Elle flinched at the sharp tone of Val's voice and moved out of Thor's grip, knowing she would receive the verbal spanking of her life.

Val leapt forward and flicked her wrist blade from its sheath. "Step away from her."

Thor didn't move. "Why?"

Val moved her blade to his throat, and again, he didn't move.

"Val." Elle's magic wound tight in her belly, and she fought to keep it there. "Val, please stop. Lord Thor said he was glad I made it home safely last night after the... the party at Lady Frigg's."

Val looked between Thor and Elle, and Elle's heart pounded. Would Val really attack Thor? What if he hurt her… what if Val hurt him? A surge of protectiveness rippled through Elle, and her magic swirled hotter, racing up her neck.

"Val, I said stop," she commanded. Elle's mouth almost fell open, realizing what she'd done. She'd never commanded Val to do anything before. Val was her friend, her confidant, and her protector; even so, Elle was the daughter of Surtr, a princess of Muspelheim. And Thor was the Norse God of Thunder. If she didn't do something, one of them was bound to be injured.

Val's gaze flicked to her, heated with disapproval and calculating her next move. Finally, she sheathed her blade back in its wrist compartment. She glared at Elle but stepped away from Thor.

"Why don't you let me buy you a drink?" Loki appeared at the top of the stairs as if strolling by. But his bright blue eyes followed the entire situation with intense interest.

Val scowled at him. "In your dreams, Playboy." She stomped to the next apartment down the hallway and stepped inside before slamming the door.

There was that word again, 'Playboy'. What did it mean?

Loki turned to Thor and shrugged. "I did my best." He winked at Elle, his gaze soft and playful, before heading back down the stairs. "Good luck, Odinson."

"What did he mean?" she asked.

Thor scratched his head, making him appear a thousand years younger. "I may have asked him to keep your friend occupied for a few minutes, so I could talk to you."

He did that for her? Her chest tightened, but her gut churned. Everything inside her fought to identify the emotions rolling through her. Curious about the way he looked at her. Fear he might find out who she was. Excitement at the thought of a gorgeous man taking interest in her. Nervousness at all the things she hid inside her that no one knew. Terror of being found by her father.

"Okay," she finally said.

His eyebrows scrunched together. "Okay?"

"I will let you pick somewhere to take me to do something, I do not know what it is, until we arrive. Preferably not involving raw fish."

His furrow deepened. "I'm not sure I understood all that, but I get the gist."

"What time are you taking me?"

"When do you get off?"

"I finish work at five."

"I'll pick you up here at six."

"Thank you."

Thor nodded and stood awkwardly for a moment. Nervousness crept up her spine. Was he changing his mind already?

"Are you going to wait here until six?" she asked.

"Uh... no. I'll come back."

She nodded. As much as she wanted him to stay, she also wanted him to leave for fear that he might change his mind. "Then you'd better go. I need to return to my shift."

"Of course." He turned and headed for the stairs, but stopped and glanced back at her.

She gave him a small wave and waited until he'd disappeared before she fell back against the wall.

A smile crossed her face and then fell. What was she doing? What was she thinking? Her gut gnawed at her insides. She had to tell Thor. She had to tell him who she was. It wasn't fair to keep that kind of secret from him.

She'd tell him tonight when he took her out. Because if they were in public on Midgard, she was relatively sure he wouldn't cause a scene in a place with so many humans… at least, she hoped that was the case.

CHAPTER SIX

The cobblestone street outside the Raven Weaver glistened with a fresh coat of rain, puddles collecting in the worn grooves between stones where centuries of foot traffic had smoothed them down. A damp chill clung to Thor's leather jacket. The kind of cold that made his knuckles ache where they'd been split and scarred over too many lifetimes to count. He straightened, rolling the tension out of his neck. Overhead, Helheim's eternal twilight pressed down, no stars, no moon, just a bruised violet sky that never quite committed to full darkness.

Ethereal lanterns lined the street, buzzing with pale-amber energy, their glow catching the mist and turning the air into something gauzy and half-real. Down the block, the low thrum of a bass line leaked out of Valhalla's Throne, and a pair of Helmarked argued in rapid-fire.

The Raven Weaver's wooden sign swung on iron hooks above the door, its carved ravens depicted in deep indigo and black, the paint fresh enough that Thor smelled linseed oil.

Thor took a deep breath and pushed open the door to the Raven Weaver. The air hit him with a heady wave of memory-laden fragrance, like standing in the grand halls of Asgard once more. It was uncanny how Frigg had perfectly captured it: the charred essence of crackling hearth fires fusing seamlessly with the rich, earthy pull of ale, while soft undertones of sweet vanilla wrapped around him like an old lullaby.

The pub's interior opened before him in tones of aged oak and deep forest green, every surface carrying the patina of deliberate care. Wrought-iron sconces shaped like twisting branches lined the walls, their flickering flames, real fire, not electric imitations, throwing copper-gold shapes across the vaulted ceiling where thick wooden beams crossed overhead like the ribs of an ancient longship. The bar itself stretched along the far wall, a massive slab of dark walnut polished to a mirror sheen, and behind it, rows of bottles caught the firelight in shades of amber, garnet, and deep honey. Thor's boots were heavy on the worn floorboards as he stepped inside, the door swinging shut behind him, muffling Helheim's ambient hum.

The air tasted faintly metallic, reminding him of mornings after battles hard-won. The good times with his brothers and friends. The bad when he'd lost people he cared about. And the worst- when Surtr had destroyed it all. He gritted his teeth and pushed the feelings aside. Tonight wasn't the night for such memories. Tonight, he had one goal in mind- find out who Elle was and why she affected him the way she did.

Each step further stirred something raw inside Thor; emotions tangled with visions unknown, felt only by those who dare traverse such mystical paths between realms and stories, mingled with destiny.

Thor walked past the rustic oak tables and chairs where various patrons drank, ate, and laughed. One by one, the patrons eyed him with wary suspicion.

When Odin suggested the move from Valhalla, Thor hadn't been sure, but honestly, he'd been more comfortable living with his demons than he ever had with the angels and fanfare in Valhalla. In Helheim, he'd found the one thing he'd always wanted- peace. And when things got too quiet, he went to Odin's fight club and took out his frustrations, usually on his dad or brothers. But occasionally, there was some other dumb soul wanting to challenge the Mighty Thor- always to their detriment.

"Thor?"

He turned before he got to the portal to Midgard.

Frigg glided toward him, her long green gown reminding him once more of the trees of Valhalla.

"Elle isn't quite done with her shift."

Thor checked his watch. Five forty-five.

"I thought she got off at five."

"She was supposed to. But Pixie didn't show up, and there's a huge crowd up there. A Midgardian football team won that yearly Super Dish thing. So the crowd is thick tonight."

"I'll wait."

"I'd be happy to pour you a drink."

"I'll wait upstairs."

Frigg looked like she wanted to say something, instead she smiled and put her hand on his arm. "Try not to start any trouble, please. The humans are worked up and celebrating. I don't want to lose business."

"Trouble? Me?"

She chuckled. "Remember how rowdy you and the warriors

three would be when you won a battle. This is the same kind of thing to the mortals. So be patient... or as patient as possible. I recently had the wooden floors redone up there, and blood is tough to remove."

Thor sighed. "Yes, Mother."

She kissed his cheek and then turned back to her deep wooden bar. Her strawberry-blonde hair intricately braided and plaited down her back. Her willowy limbs worked to pour mugs of ale and set them on the bar for the waitress to deliver. He had no idea how she didn't tire of serving people all day, every day. But he supposed serving in the pub was to her what working on motorcycles was to him. A way to pass the time.

Thor turned back to the portal and stepped through.

Elle glanced at the clock. Five fifty. Thor would arrive any minute, but she couldn't bail on Val and Kirsten. The mortals were more obnoxious than she'd seen them before. She'd stopped counting the number of fake compliments thrown her way meant to flatter her into speaking to the various men. She wondered if all mortals thought stupid lines like- *'Somebody call the cops because it's got to be illegal to look that good!'* And *'Hey girl, are you a beaver? Cause damn!'* And worst of all, *'Is that a mirror in your pocket? Cause I can see myself in your pants.'*- were intelligent ways for a man to attract a woman's attention. She wasn't sure what the last one meant, but she didn't want to ask either.

Elle dropped off another round of beers to a corner booth full of guys and girls whose faces had been painted blue and white. One guy wore no shirt but had painted a blue number 42 on his chest. Elle couldn't understand the obsession with adult men playing a silly ball game- especially by people they didn't know.

Over the last weeks, she'd come to understand mortals had many fascinations she didn't understand. One was football. Another game called soccer, though she thought those names should be switched. She also didn't understand their fascination with shiny, sleek automobiles and music whose lyrics made no sense. But the strangest of all was on Wednesday nights when patrons would become quite inebriated and sing badly in front of everyone at the pub. Why in the world they would embarrass themselves, she had no idea. She herself sang well but had no desire to do so in front of a crowd.

Elle set her tray on the bar, and Val shoved another tray toward her without looking.

"Table sixteen."

Elle's gut clenched every time Val refused to meet her eye. Val remained angry about Thor more than about Elle telling her to back off. Elle knew Val was only mad because she was scared for both of them. Even so, Elle tired of being treated like a sheltered child. They had come to Midgard to leave that behind. If she couldn't build some sort of life for herself, what was the point of leaving their prison? The only things she'd done since arriving were work at the pub, read in her room, and sleep. Aside from the strange party at Frigg's, she'd basically done the same things she had back home- minus the abuse.

Elle lifted the tray and walked toward table sixteen.

Thor stepped out from behind the curtain which hid the staircase and portal to Helheim. Her body flushed with heat at the sight of his handsome face, and she turned away.

She set the drinks down on table sixteen to endure another round of stupid comments aimed at her beauty and body.

"Enjoy." She threw a tight smile.

She turned to head back to the bar when a pair of arms wrapped around her waist and pulled her onto the lap of one of the rowdy men.

"I'll enjoy it much better if you sit with me while I drink," he said.

Stunned, Elle couldn't move; like when Thadren put his hand on her thigh, and her brain froze. All the lessons with Val, teaching her to fight and trying to harness her gift, and there she sat, unable to think straight, with the exception of her magic, which flared inside her in defense.

"I would enjoy that too," said another guy at the table.

"What about me?" said a third male. "I don't mind being third."

Every fiber of Elle's body went rigid. Val finished pouring a beer and spotted her. Her jaw tightened, and she hopped over the bar in one swift movement, but she was too slow.

A blur of black leather appeared in front of Elle, and before she processed what had happened, she stood behind Thor, and he had the man's face smashed into the table-top, arm wrenched behind him.

"Whoa!" The guy's buddies at the table backed up.

Thor turned to Elle. "Did he ask permission to touch you?"

Elle hugged her tray close to her chest and shook her head. Thor's eyes flashed white with lightning, and he turned back to the whimpering man with his cheek jammed into a plate of fries.

"What gives you the right to touch a woman without her permission?"

"I... I... was only playing."

"Playing?" Thor grabbed the back of the man's head and whipped it up so the man looked at Elle. "Does she look like she thought it was funny?"

Elle's gaze dropped at the sight of fries and ketchup stuck to the side of the man's head.

"N...no," the man stammered.

"Apologize," Thor demanded.

"I'm sorry," the man muttered.

Thor wrenched his arm further behind his back, and the man cried out. "I don't think she heard you."

"I'm sorry," the guy said louder.

"He's sorry," said another guy. "We all are."

Elle lifted her eyes. "Thor, it's okay."

He studied her, conflicted for a moment, and then dropped the guy back on the table before going to her and grasping her arm.

Behind him, her table of drunk troublemakers rushed from the bar, leaving a substantial tip behind.

"It's not okay, Elle," Thor said. "No one should ever touch you without your permission." He searched her face, making sure she understood.

Her fingers twitched, and her gut twisted as the desire to run surfaced quicker than it had in weeks.

"Even you?" she asked, knowing he'd touched her several times already without asking.

He dropped his hand, making her skin cool. "Even me. I apologize."

She wanted to tell him it was okay, but she didn't think he would like that answer.

"Why don't you put your tray up, and we can go?"

"But I haven't showered or changed clothes."

He nodded. "Plan changed. The new plan works best with what you are wearing."

She inspected her Raven Weaver T-shirt, black leggings, and sneakers. She didn't want to go out with Thor wearing work clothes.

"All right." She turned to the bar as the other patrons eyed her and Thor.

"Elle?" Thor took a step forward.

She turned, and he leaned into her ear. "Hold your head up. Make eye contact with people. It's the only way they will respect you."

Hold her head up? Make eye contact? He sounded like Val. The idea was simple enough, but when it'd been beaten into her for longer than she could remember, that doing those things would earn her a thrashing, she didn't know how to.

She lifted her eyes and swallowed hard as she walked to the bar and set down her tray.

Val still hadn't returned to the other side of the bar. "You good?"

Elle nodded.

Val looked like she might say something more. Instead, she jumped back over in one fluid movement.

Kirsten walked to Elle. "Why don't you take off. You've had a long shift. I'll be fine until Merda arrives."

"Are you sure?" Elle asked.

"She'll be here in thirty. I can handle these morons. They're not stupid enough to be handsy with me." Kirsten winked at her.

"What makes you different?"

"When I first started working here, my brother made his presence known for the first month on every one of my shifts. He's a Hell's Angel. No one messes with Hell's Angels."

Elle's brows scrunched together. "I thought angels in hel were called Helborn."

Kirsten burst into a laugh. "You're funny. I love you, girl."

Elle wasn't sure what she'd said that was funny.

CHAPTER SEVEN

"Where are we going?"

Thor walked through the portal back to Helheim with Elle in tow. They stepped into the Helheim side of The Raven Weaver, and Thor led Elle through the throng of immortals and Helmarked- those marked by Hel to remain in her realm and serve her. The immortals glanced at him but turned away. But the Helmarked stared at Elle, their hungry eyes devouring her every step. They who could never leave unless commanded to by Hel. Thor rounded the bar, and Elle pressed closer to him. He fought the urge to take her hand or put his arm around her. He told himself it would only be for her safety, but he couldn't lie. He would be doing it to make himself feel better, and to make sure all the Helmarked knew she wasn't to be messed with. Not unless they wanted to deal with him.

They made their way to the exterior door, and he opened it. She paused and bit her lip before stepping into the muggy, dim light.

Once outside, Thor again fought the urge to take her hand.

"Are we going to Lady Frigg's?"

"No," he said. "I was going to take you to one of my favorite places to eat, but I decided there was something more pressing we needed to do."

"More pressing?"

He looked at her angelic face, the soft glow of street lamps catching on the delicate curve of her cheek. Her expression was a tempest of emotions, a balance between trust and terror. Her wide eyes glistened, reflecting both the flickering light and the unspoken anxiety that churned within her. The soft rise and fall of her chest betrayed her rapid breathing, though she tried to steady herself, holding his gaze as if tethering herself to him.

Even in something as unremarkable as a plain black shirt and worn leggings, her effortless beauty was breathtaking in its simplicity. The shirt clung to her frame, dampened by sweat, outlining the gentle slope of her shoulders and the curve of her waist. Her leggings were speckled with pretzel crumbs and smudges from their hurried escape. It wasn't what she wore, but how she wore it. Raw and real, stripped of pretense, like a masterpiece left unfinished yet more profound for its imperfections.

"Elle, you need to learn to take care of yourself. Both in Midgard and Helheim," he said. "If you don't, you'll be eaten alive."

Her eyes widened.

"Not literally... well, at least not on Midgard. Down here, anything is possible."

She scanned the area, as if waiting for someone to jump out and attack her. She wrapped her arms around herself and shivered.

"Are you cold?"

She nodded.

"I've been here so long I forget most immortals visiting aren't used to the cold." He shrugged out of his leather jacket and draped it over her shoulders.

Thor took her hand and rounded a corner on autopilot. He'd made the trip so many times from the Raven Weaver to his home that he'd done it blind drunk in the past.

They rounded another corner, and he slowed as his shop came into view.

Elle slowed. "A closed business?"

"It's mine. I fix and build motorcycles. I have an apartment upstairs."

"Oh," she paused for a moment. "What's a motorcycle?"

He looked back at her. She really had been sheltered. "An automatic bike which has a motor on it so you don't have to pedal."

Thor stopped outside the door of his shop.

Elle noticed his sign and smiled. "Mjölnir Motors."

The way she said it surprised Thor. Her pronunciation spot on. He'd never met anyone outside of Asgard who pronounced it correctly. And most of the people there couldn't do it.

He opened the door, flipped on the lights, and they walked onto the shop floor.

A row of vintage motorcycle frames hung along the far wall on iron hooks, their metal bones stripped down to raw steel, each one tagged with a handwritten work order in Thor's blocky script. Below them, a long steel workbench ran the length of the shop, cluttered with socket wrenches, torque gauges, and a half-empty mug of black coffee gone cold hours ago. The air tasted like motor oil and old rubber. Overhead, industrial pendant lamps buzzed against exposed ductwork, their glow bouncing off the polished floor in pale squares. Outside, a steady breeze drummed against the roll-up garage door. A partially rebuilt V-twin engine sat exposed on the center lift, its cylinder heads removed and laid out on a shop rag in precise order-crankcase, pistons, valve springs- each piece gleaming with fresh oil. He gritted his teeth, realizing he'd forgotten to put down a tarp to catch any drips from ruining his floor. He hated not finishing a job.

"You don't lock your door?" Elle asked.

"No reason. No one here would dare come in without permission."

She smiled. "Guess everyone is scared of you."

He wasn't sure what his expression showed, but her smile fell, making him want to punch himself for having upset her.

"I'm sorry," she said.

What the hell was wrong with him?

"Come on." He took her hand and led her across the floor as he headed for the backroom. She shrugged off his leather coat and handed it to him. He hung it on a wall hook.

"Are these your motorbikes?" She ran her fingers over his favorite bike, making his jeans grow tight as he imagined her fingers running over his skin instead.

He coughed, trying to cool himself down. "Yeah. One is called Tanngrisnir, and the other is Tanngnjóstr."

Her eyebrows drew together for a moment. "Wait. You turned your two beloved goats into motorcycles?"

He folded his arms over his chest. "You sure do know a lot about me."

"Well..."

The flustered expression on her face made Thor smile. Could she be more adorable?

Whoa! Adorable? Since when had he ever called anyone adorable? More than that, since when had he ever liked anything because it was adorable?

"It... It's not hard to find out about a Norse god. The legends are, well, legendary. I mean, how many books, stories, and movies have they made with you in them? A million?"

"So, you learned about me through watching actors pretend to be me for entertainment?"

"I prefer to read. Back... where I'm from, I had a huge library. I read all kinds of things. Like how you would eat your goats when you got hungry."

Thor gritted his teeth. "I ate them one time. One. And the whole thing got blown way out of proportion. They made it sound like I did it all the time. And I will have you know, Tanngrisnir and Tanngnjóstr begged me to eat them. They said if I starved to death, they didn't want to belong to anyone else. They begged me to eat them and not die."

"Did they beg you to cause one of them a limp, too?" she chided.

"That was all Loki. Idiot. He convinced a boy to mess with Tanngnjóstr's bones after dinner. I didn't find out until it was too late."

A mischievous smile spread across her face.

"You're messing with me." Man, how did she rile him up? And in more ways than one.

"I'm not sure what that means, but I am jesting with you. But you haven't answered my question. Did you?"

"Did I what?"

"Did you turn Tanngrisnir and Tanngnjóstr into motorcycles?"

Again, her pronunciation correct. He shook his head and walked to the back of the shop floor, opened a door, and motioned her forward. He stepped into his fight room. As soon as he did, a series of loud bleats sounded from the corner.

"Yeah, I hear you, you noisy beasts."

Elle squealed in delight. "You didn't turn them into machines." She ran to the pen where Tanngrisnir and Tanngnjóstr stood on their hind legs begging for food.

Before he warned her, they didn't like people; she was at their pen, grabbing them by the face and kissing them. Thor stopped mid-step, processing the scene. Tanngrisnir and Tanngnjóstr didn't like anyone. After thousands of years, they tolerated him at best. But there they were, hamming it up and licking Elle all over her face like she was the best bale of hay he'd ever given them.

He stared in disbelief for several minutes, listening to her coo and laugh at the goats while they nipped at her shirt and fought each other for her attention.

What in the Helheim is it about that girl?

Thor scooped some pellets from the ancient barrel and dropped them into their trough.

"All right, guys, back up. Give the woman some air." He pushed the goats down, and Tanngrisnir nipped his arm.

"Hey!" Thor pointed at the goat. "I'll eat you again. I will."

The goats backed up and snorted several times, stamping their feet like they might try to ram the gate.

"You wouldn't really eat them, would you?" Elle asked, her voice barely a whisper.

Thor snorted and tossed the scoop back in the barrel. "Probably not. They didn't taste good the first time. They're a thousand years older now. They'd probably mold instantly upon death."

The goats bleated again and began munching on their pellets.

"Is this why you brought me here? To show me your goats?"

"Nope. I brought you here to teach you some self-defense."

"Self-defense?"

"Yeah. You need to be able to defend yourself against assholes like the guy who grabbed you."

Her eyebrows scrunched together.

"It's a figure of speech. It means... a... uh..." Thor wasn't sure how to describe an asshole without being graphic. "A not nice guy."

She nodded, but a nervous expression crossed her face.

"Don't worry. I won't hurt you. I just want you to be able to protect yourself so you don't find yourself in the same situation again."

She swallowed hard. "All right."

THE ROOM SPREAD BEFORE HER, A CAVERNOUS EXPANSE THAT stretched endlessly, cloaked in an oppressive monotony of dull gray. The walls bore no adornments, no hint of life or personality, just the cold, industrial chill of utilitarian design. Their smooth, unyielding surface reflected the faint sheen of the overhead lights, though the glow itself felt muted, swallowed by the space's lifelessness. Beneath his boots, the floor mirrored this same stark grayness, its hard texture echoing with each step he took.

In the corner of this desolate scene stood the only break in uniformity- the dark wooden enclosure. Its rich mahogany tones stood out defiantly against the drab surroundings. The sturdy planks formed a pen, their edges worn smooth by time and use. Inside, Tanngrisnir and Tanngnjóstr shuffled, their hooves clicking against the wood. The scents of metal mingled with the smell of fresh hay and the pellets the goats ate.

She wasn't sure what to say about him wanting to teach her self-defense. If she told him Val was a Valkyrie and had taught her to fight for years, he would become suspicious and wonder why she hadn't defended herself earlier. But how did she tell him she knew how to fight without telling him why she didn't fight back? About how the beatings and abuse at her father's hands caused her freeze response to take over every inch of her body, almost any time someone touched her.

But… maybe self-defense was different from fighting. Maybe she might actually learn how to stick up for herself.

Thor walked to a corner, pulled several large red items out, and dropped them onto the floor before unfolding them and laying them out.

"Come over to the mats." He motioned her over.

"Should I remove my shoes?"

He shook his head. "You need to be wearing whatever you might be wearing if someone tries to touch you without your permission again. That way, you will feel most familiar when it happens."

She stepped on the springy mats. She bounced on the balls of her feet and crossed to Thor and stopped.

Thor thought for a moment. "To do this, I'm gonna have to touch you, all right?"

Her throat dried, but she nodded.

"First, I want to do what happened to you earlier. I'm gonna grab you around the waist." He waited.

He what? He was going to wrap his body around her body. Touch her?

Her heartbeat kicked up, and a trickle of fear dripped down her back. Her core warmed as her magic pulsed inside her, ready to defend like always. She took in a deep, slow, calming breath. She could do this. She could do this. No magic explosions. No, letting him see her true nature. She had to learn control. If she couldn't control it in front of the one person she needed to most, then what chance did she have of learning to use it at all?

She turned away from him, and he approached. Her heartbeat galloped as his warm breath tickled her skin and made it pebble. He brushed the hair from her neck, and she swallowed hard as her limbs shook. Her magic flared, but she pulled it back, shoving it down.

He wrapped his arms around her waist and applied gentle pressure. "Where were your arms when he grabbed you?"

Tanngrisnir and Tanngnjóstr bleated and jumped at the fencing of their pen.

"Knock it off. I'm not going to hurt her," Thor called.

Tanngrisnir and Tanngnjóstr continued to bleat, unconvinced.

"You know I won't hurt you, right?"

She wanted to say yes, but she couldn't. It was a lie. If he found out the truth about who she was, she had no idea what he would do.

His arms loosened. "I won't hurt you, Elle. We don't have to do this if-"

She shook her head. "No… I want to. I… need to."

Tanngrisnir and Tanngnjóstr kicked at the gate to their enclosure.

Thor snorted. “Maybe you should tell them you’re fine. They don’t believe me.”

Elle looked at the goats as they began trying to climb out. “I’m okay, guys. I’m okay.”

They both stood on their hind legs, looking over the edge of their pen like protective older brothers.

Thor snorted. “I’ve had them for centuries, and yet they worry more for your safety than mine. I’m not sure how I feel about that.”

“Maybe it’s because they’ve read the stories about you.”

Thor didn’t move for a moment, and then he burst into a deep booming laugh that made her smile.

“That was a good one. You’re witty. I like that.”

The tension between them eased, and she relaxed.

“All right, you ready?”

She had no idea, but she nodded anyway.

Thor's powerful arms enveloped her waist once more, and a wave of warmth surged through her that had nothing to do with her magic. Her thoughts muddied with sensations she'd never encountered. An intense heat suffused her skin, while her stomach danced. Not anxiety. Something altogether different.

The low rumble of his breath resonated in the silence, rhythmic like distant thunder. The press of him against her back solid and reassuring.

A scent lingered around them. The fresh aroma reminiscent of rain-soaked earth mingled with a hint of ozone.

Thor said something, and she cleared her thoughts and focused on what they were doing.

“What?”

“Where were your arms when he grabbed you?”

"Uh..." *Concentrate girl. He'll think you're an idiot if you can't keep your head while he is trying to teach you.* "In front of me."

"And what were you holding?"

"The tray."

"Right. You have options, but I'm gonna teach you a few of the easiest."

Her heart pounded so hard she was sure he felt it through her back. He tightened his hold like hardbound ropes. His warm chest hit her back as her body relaxed into him.

For a moment, wave after wave of warmth crashed over her like the heated waves of the ocean back home.

"Ready?" Thor asked close to her ear.

She nodded, trying to gain control of her mind and body.

"First, throw your head back and smash me in the face," said Thor. "A broken nose is a great way to make someone let go of you. Try it."

She shook her head. "I don't want to hurt you."

"Trust me. I'll dodge. But the guy grabbing you won't because he won't expect it. Go on. Throw your head back hard and quick."

Elle closed her eyes and leaned her head back until it rested on his shoulder.

"Uh... no," he said. "You aren't using me as a pillow. Faster and harder. If you do it like that, they are more likely to think you are enjoying it."

Elle took a deep breath and tried again. This time, she whipped her head back and caught Thor on the right cheek.

"I'm sorry," she said. "I'm sorry."

"No," said Thor. "No, that was perfect. You're faster than I thought you'd be."

She peeked over her shoulder. "Are you okay?"

"I'm fine. Though if I'd been a fraction slower, I'd have a broken nose right now. Well done."

He smiled, and her heart squeezed. It was a genuine, broad, toothy smile that made her smile in return. She liked the way his eyes crinkled when he smiled. And she noticed a dimple she'd not seen before. Every moment she looked at him, he grew more and more handsome. How was that possible?

"All right. So, if someone grabs you, the first thing you can do is throw your head back. The second option is to use your elbow or the tray in your hand. Like with your head, you can throw your elbow back and catch the guy in the nose, eye, throat, ribs, it doesn't matter. Any of those hits will make him let go."

"But... won't it make him angry? Won't he strike me?"

"Not if he knows what's good for him." Thor's eyes flashed with deadly lightning.

"You need to stop being scared of what they might do to you if you fight back and worry more about what they might do to you if you don't."

Elle knew all too well what happened when she didn't fight back. She'd had the bruises, cuts, and welts to prove it at one time or another.

Val had brought her to Midgard to become a new person. The person she wanted to be. And the person she wanted to be was strong. So fighting back was something she needed to learn.

"Here." Thor turned her to face him and put his hand on her shoulder. "Push my hands off and tell me no."

She brushed his hand away. "No, thank you."

Thor shook his head. "Say it forcefully. And don't say thank you. Tell me no."

She took a deep breath and pushed his hand a bit harder. "No."

"I didn't believe you for a minute." He put both hands on her shoulders. "Push my hand off and say, 'Don't touch me'."

She pushed his hand. "Please, don't touch me."

"No!" His voice rose, making her jump. "There. That right there, that's the problem. You're scared of everything."

Elle dropped her gaze. She didn't want to look weak in front of him. But she wasn't sure what he would do if she showed him what she was fully capable of.

A moment passed, and then Thor tilted her chin up.

"Someone hurt you."

She swallowed hard as her eyes filled with tears. Memories flooded her.

The time her father found her sneaking food from the kitchen, and had forced it all into her mouth at once, causing her to choke until she threw up. Then he'd thrown her to the ground and made her clean it up with her bare hands. The time he'd told her to dance for his men and when she hadn't, he'd kicked her to the floor. The time one of his men had grabbed her, and her father had laughed at her, letting him grope her instead of helping her.

"Elle?"

Tanngrisnir and Tanngnjóstr kicked and bleated again, pulling her from her thoughts.

Her gaze whipped up as the memories faded. Thor's eyes flashed silver again, and he pulled her into his arms. His soft T-shirt pressed against her cheek, and she couldn't help but wrap her arms around his back and cling to him.

She'd never talked about the abuse. Not even with Val. Everyone in the kingdom knew what she'd suffered, but no one said anything. No one did anything. Only Val had taken to teaching her to fight. Aside from that, no one in her father's kingdom had cared.

A moment passed, and she relaxed into him, the sensation

strange. For the first time in her life, she felt safe. Like no matter what happened, she would be protected… but there was something more… something deeper…

"All right," said Thor. "Let's start differently. What is the worst thing that could happen if you fight back?"

"They could hurt me," she said.

"But you've been hurt before. Being hurt is horrible, but you've lived through it, and so you know what that feels like, and now you don't want to feel it again, correct?"

"True." She never admitted it to anyone before.

"Now it's time to make sure you have the tools you need to keep it from happening again. What if by fighting back, you can keep it from happening again? Wouldn't that be worth it, knowing if you do nothing, you will definitely be hurt?"

"You're right."

"Okay, so, the first thing is to make sure you know you deserve better and are able to tell someone no, and mean it, and have them listen. Now, tell me no, and push away from me and mean it."

Elle chewed her lip. "No." She tried to push from his grip, but he held her fast. "It didn't work."

Thor glowered at her. "Did you mean it?"

"N... no," she stammered. "I like it when you hug me." The words tumbled from her mouth before she stopped them. Her cheeks heated.

Thor's eyebrows rose, and something changed between them. Suddenly, heat sparked her skin once more. Thor's hand splayed on her back, sending warmth down her thighs.

He leaned in, and Elle's heart beat so fast she thought she might pass out. His lips moved closer to hers, and she sucked in a breath and held it.

Kiss her. Was he going to-

Before she finished the thought, his lips pressed to hers lightly. He pulled her closer, and she gripped the back of his shirt.

Kissed. She was being kissed. For the first time in her life. And by Thor, God of Thunder.

His lips pressed harder against hers and parted them. The tip of his tongue licked her bottom lip, making her gasp.

He pulled away. "I'm sorry. I shouldn't have."

"Why?"

"Because I am trying to teach you to stand up for yourself and be assertive, and I go and kiss you. I apologize."

"No," she said.

His brow creased. "No?"

"I don't want you to apologize. I don't want you to be sorry."

A smile curved his lips. "Now if only you'd be that forceful when you're telling a different man not to touch you."

She smiled.

Thor picked up the locket she hadn't realized had slipped out of her shirt.

"What's this?"

Elle plucked it from his fingers. "A locket I made. It has my mother's portrait in it."

Thor touched the locket again. "You made this?"

She nodded. "With my own two hands."

He stared at it for a moment. "It's beautifully crafted. How did you learn to make it?"

"I... uh... I taught myself. I picked up metal scraps and... just made it."

He stared at it for a moment. "Have you made anything else?"

She shrugged. "A few things, but nothing with this complexity. The hinge was especially difficult to get right."

He inspected the locket. "You could sell things like this."

"Really?" She loved creating jewelry and working with gems. Would people want to buy her work?

"If you taught yourself to make something like this and it's one of your first tries, you have quite a gift."

Elle smiled and put the locket back into her shirt. A talent. She had a talent. It was the first time anyone had said that.

CHAPTER EIGHT

Thor could not figure Elle out. One moment, he was afraid she might break from a stern look, and the next, he witnessed a fire inside her which made every inch of him wake up.

Holding her in his arms, he was once again struck by how warm her skin was to the touch. He wondered if it was his imagination or if she truly radiated heat. And his goats… what the hel was with them wanting to protect her from him?

He stared into her beautiful eyes, wanting nothing more than to take her up to his bed and make love to her.

Whoa! Where had that come from?

"So." He cleared his throat. "We should return to helping you stick up for yourself."

She nodded, and a serious expression crossed her face. "Yes. I need to learn to defend myself. I've never simply defended before."

He wondered what she meant, but before he could ask, the back door opened, and his father walked in.

"Thor, I was wondering-" Odin stopped, his eyes widening. He looked from Elle to Thor and back again.

"Yes?" Thor asked, trying to keep irritation from his voice. “Come right in.”

Odin continued to stare at Elle and then coughed. "Sorry. Where are my manners?" He walked forward and extended his hand.

Elle glanced at Thor and shook Odin's hand. "Elle."

"Elle." Odin rolled the word around as if mulling something over, while continuing to shake her hand. Finally, Odin leaned in and kissed Elle's knuckles. "Lady Elle, it's a pleasure to see you again."

Elle pulled away.

"Again?" asked Thor. "You've met Elle before?"

Odin's gaze narrowed.

"Yes," said Elle. “At the Raven Weaver. Lady Frigg introduced us."

Odin nodded and smiled. "Frigg has always liked to take people in and make sure they are cared for."

“I thought you only drank at your club,” Thor said.

Odin shrugged. “Usually.”

Something about the way Odin kept looking at Elle set Thor on edge. He couldn't put his finger on it, but he didn't like it.

"Did you need something, Father?"

Odin finally looked at Thor for the first time and smiled. "I came because I wanted to tell you everyone is back. We are going to have a family dinner at my place, Friday night."

Thor nodded.

Odin smiled. “I’ll let you two do whatever you were doing."

"I'm teaching her how to defend herself."

A soft expression crossed over Odin's face. "A person should never be subject to the abuse of others. Especially a beautiful young woman." Odin bowed to Elle. "I hope you will join us for dinner on Friday."

"Th... Thank you, Lord Odin." She curtsied so fluidly Thor almost imagined seeing her in a royal court. "I am not sure if I am available, but I sincerely appreciate the invitation."

Odin left without another word, and a tense silence fell between Thor and Elle.

She turned back to him. "What's next?"

He studied her for a moment. The way she stood at the ready. Her stance strong and balanced. "You've been taught to fight, haven't you?"

Elle swallowed, and her smile fell a bit. "Some."

"More than some, I think."

She shrugged.

"If you've been taught to fight, why didn't you fight back when the man grabbed you?"

"There is a difference between fighting off an attacker and defending yourself from someone you think means you no harm to begin with."

Thor nodded. "True."

"If you came at me intent on punching me in the face, or stabbing me with a sword, or trying to kill me, it would be different. Those are attacks I am used to fighting off. But... It's like you said. I should keep my shoes on because it helps me feel like I will when things happen to me. I was taught to fight, but only wearing fighting clothes. Only in one room. Only with one person. So, it didn't feel the same. When he put his arms around me, I wasn't trained for that, so I froze. Plus..."

"Plus, what?"

"He's mortal. Things are different on Midgard. I can't grab a sword without causing a lot of people, including Lady Frigg, who has done so much to help me, a lot of problems."

She wasn't wrong. Thor had learned that the hard way. His record with the Midgard police would be at least a dozen pages long if Loki hadn't helped.

"Show me," he said.

"Show you what?"

"What you've learned."

"You want me to fight you?"

"Sure. I'll go easy on you. And I promise not to use Mjölnir."

She chuckled. "What's the fun in that?"

Thor and Elle sparred for thirty minutes, and he had to admit how impressed he was at her skill. But more than the level of her skill was the technique she'd been taught. A technique he'd seen thousands of times before.

Thor walked to the fridge. "Where are you from?"

"You know where I live."

He opened the fridge, pulled out two bottles of water, and walked back to her.

"No. I mean, before that. Before coming to the Midgard and Helheim. Where were you before? You have to be an immortal or paranormal of some kind. It's obvious you are hiding from someone or someones. Are you another god? Greek? Roman? You don't look Egyptian or Asian. And your fighting style is Asgardian. Why is that?"

Elle's eyes rang with fear. She took several gulps of the water and sucked in a breath. "I'm from one of the nine realms."

"You're Asgardian?"

"Yes and no. My mother was a priestess. A sorceress, like your mother. In fact, they were friends for a long time, I am told. But my father was not Asgardian."

He studied her face, trying to see if any of her features were familiar. "Frigg knew your mother? How did we never meet?"

"It was quite a long time ago. I wasn't born yet, and when my mother... met my father..." She trailed off and sipped her water.

Thor caught the tension in her stance as she spoke about her parents. Maybe it was something she was ashamed of. "So, your mother was a sorceress. Did she teach you anything?"

Her eyes saddened. "I never met her. She died in childbirth."

Thor's chest squeezed. "I'm sorry." Dammit, why was he being so nosy?

"Me too."

"Who taught you to fight? And how did they learn the Asgardian style?"

She gave him a weak smile. "You know I've kind of had a long day, and I'm rather tired. Do you mind if we continue this lesson a different day?"

"Of course," Thor said, attempting to keep the disappointment from his voice.

Guilt washed through him. Go slow, that's what Frigg had said. Thor had pushed her further than she was comfortable, but his curiosity couldn't be curbed. He wanted to know everything about her.

A million questions blasted through Thor's mind, but in the end, he only came to one conclusion- there was something she was hiding from him. Something that scared her. Something she didn't want anyone to know. But how many of the other immortals in

Helheim couldn't say they were running from something? Not many. He needed to let it go.

She watched him intently and bit her lower lip, making his body heat. He remembered the feel of her in his arms. Her heated skin. The shallow breaths she took at his touch. He wanted to feel that again. Wanted to taste her berry-colored lips. Wanted to run his hands through her soft, long tresses and cradle her against him. His need to protect and worship her became all-consuming. His jeans grew tight around him, and he turned from her enticing gaze and gulped down his water. He needed to get it together. He was supposed to be teaching her to defend herself, not hit on her like a bar wench.

Elle walked off the mats shakily and went over to pet Tanngrisnir and Tanngnjóstr. The heat in Thor's eyes had almost been more than she could bear. It had made her want to throw herself against him and feel his solid arms around her again. She needed to stop. Needed to get it together. He was helping her. Being nice to her, and that's all it could be between them. Nothing more. No matter how beautiful his icy blue eyes were. Or how he filled out a leather coat perfectly. Or how he smelled of leather and metal. A scent that back on Muspelheim she would have hated. But on him it was utterly enthralling.

Thor joined her, took her empty water bottle, and tossed it in the trash.

Now. Now is when I should tell him who I am. He deserves to know.

But for the first time in her long life, she actually felt cared for, peaceful, and safe. She didn't want to ruin that. What would happen if she told him?

Her hands shook, and her stomach growled so loud everyone in Helheim had probably heard it. She grabbed her stomach as it cramped.

"Odin's beard," said Thor. "When was the last time you ate, woman?"

Elle thought for a moment. "I'm not much of a cook. I ate cereal before my shift started."

Thor shook his head. "This morning? The last time you ate was this morning? You're lucky you haven't passed out by now. I should have realized. I'm sorry. Let me grab you dinner."

"You don't need to. I have food in my loft."

"Cereal?" His eyebrow cocked upward.

Busted. "I like cereal." She'd bought a dozen different kinds at the mortal store on Midgard. She liked the one with the leprechaun on it best. She always saved the little marshmallows for last. She liked the one that tasted like chocolate and peanut butter, too.

"Well, you need more than cereal to keep you going at Frigg's place. And fending off those jerks you have to deal with. Let me take you to my favorite place to eat down here."

Part of her wanted to go, but a larger part of her swirled with guilt. She was lying to Thor on purpose, and she didn't want to. She wanted to be honest with him. Tell him everything. Maybe he would be okay with it. Maybe he would want to protect her from her father… But what if he didn't? What if instead of looking at her like she was fascinating, he looked at her with rage, disgust, and loathing? She wasn't sure her heart could handle it. Not after everything she'd been through.

"Not tonight," she said finally.

Thor nodded. "Rain check?"

She thought for a moment, trying to process his words. "We need to check for rain?"

"No. A rain check means a different day."

Why? "Oh. Yes. A rain check then."

Thor stared at her for a moment and motioned her forward. "Let's get you to your cereal."

THEY WALKED TO THE RAVEN WEAVER IN SILENCE. ELLE'S conscience screamed at her for not telling him. The whole walk, she had tried to psych herself up, but as the words presented themselves on her tongue, she couldn't. Something inside stopped her.

She didn't want to lie to Thor, but she didn't want to lose him either. They'd only seen each other a few times, and yet she'd experienced a connection with him she'd never had with another person. Something of her own. Something only for her. Something she was sure she'd never share with anyone else.

Thor guided her past an alley, and an icy shiver darted up Elle's spine. She paused to scan the silent street behind them. A hush blanketed the area, almost tangible in its stillness. The muffled buzz of voices seeped out of Frigg's place three blocks away.

“Are you okay?” Thor asked.

Elle turned towards him.

“What's wrong?” he continued, reaching into his coat pocket and withdrawing a heavy, ancient-looking hammer.

“I... I don't know,” she replied.

They moved together, inspecting each building. Elle stilled her breath, ears straining for movement.

Something creaked amidst the shadows. Thor tensed beside her; instinctively, she clutched at his arm.

"It's nothing," he reassured. "Probably some helspawn skulking around for easy prey. Let's head inside."

His eyes flickered between her and the looming structures she'd been wary of. He wrapped his arm around her waist, solid and warm, and nudged her toward The Raven Weaver's comforting glow.

Even so, Elle noticed he didn't holster his hammer back in his coat.

Each step carried them closer toward sanctuary, leaving behind whispers and possible enemies veiled in the gloom.

When they reached the entrance to Frigg's bar, it felt like coming up for air after being under the bath water too long. The warmth and spices from inside hit her when Thor opened the door, and her body relaxed. She was safe. Nothing would hurt her in the Raven Weaver. Neither Thor nor Lady Frigg would allow it.

They walked halfway through the bar, surprised to find Val sitting with Loki.

Loki spotted them, and Val turned. Her gaze narrowed, and she stood, but Elle gave her a small smile, and Val stopped. Loki said something to her, and she sat back down.

She and Thor continued through the portal and up through the topside of the Raven Weaver to the lofts above. They'd reached her door before Thor put his hammer away, and the tension in his body subsided. Though he'd said whatever had made her nervous was probably nothing, his aura said otherwise.

She pushed her hair behind her ears. "Thank you for showing me your place."

He nodded. "It wasn't how I'd expected tonight to go."

"We'll have to try again." Man, she was getting bold. But somehow being with him made her bold. Strong.

"How about tomorrow? I will take you to the restaurant I like."

The memory of the alleyway came back.

"In Helheim?" She wasn't sure she wanted to go back so soon.

"No. Up here."

Elle licked her lips. She hadn't dared to venture out anywhere besides the block the Raven Weaver occupied. "Okay."

Thor nodded. "Good."

"What should I wear?"

"Whatever you want. But definitely pants."

She nodded. "Til tomorrow night, then."

"Tomorrow." He didn't move.

Neither did she.

Elle's heartbeat echoed in her ears, a relentless drum. Her eyes flickered to his lips before she willed them upward, meeting his intense, unyielding gaze, then glanced away, heat rising in her cheeks. Thor's jaw clenched; she caught the quiet rasp of his breath. His hand hovered near hers.

Neither moved closer; neither broke the fragile tension. The space between them felt like a living thing- taut and electric.

Don't reach for him. Don't let desire consume you. Remember who you are. Who your father is.

He nodded and turned to leave. But before he stepped away, their eyes locked once more- a fleeting exchange which burned bright and urgent.

Her fingers twitched towards him, but she held back, biting her lip to stop the longing surging inside her.

Elle touched her pocket and shook her head. "I think I left my keys downstairs at the bar."

Thor gripped the door handle. "I can open it for you."

"No, don't break-"

As the door creaked open unexpectedly, a shiver ran down her spine.

"Looks like you forgot to lock it."

Elle peered into a place always so familiar yet now wrapped in an unsettling chill. Forgetting to lock the door was unlike her. She retraced her steps from earlier that day. The hallway light spilled into the room, casting long shadows that danced across the floor.

"Want me to check if everything's okay?" His voice calm and steady as ever.

The subtle scent of vanilla lingered in the air, the candles she'd burned before work. A cool draft brushed past, making her skin prickle.

She shook her head. "No," she replied, feeling the steady thump of anticipation like drumbeats in her chest. "I'm sure you're right."

Elle stepped inside. Again, a chill raced over her, but nothing moved. She flicked on the lamp and did a quick inventory of the room, and nothing seemed out of place. The modest-sized space above the Raven Weaver sported a kitchenette tucked into one corner and a small bedroom with a large, comfortable bed against the far wall. Frigg had set it up for her when she'd first arrived, and Elle had done what she could with it since. The walls were bare of pictures, but the soft, creamy color warmed the entire space. A large wooden bookcase with books filling every inch. A half-finished copper bracelet sat on the kitchen table beside a pair of needle-nose pliers. The whole place smelled like the pub below-old wood and ale- mixed with the vanilla aroma of her favorite candle.

"Are you sure you're alright?"

Elle spun around and threw a smile on her face. "Yes, thank you. I'm being silly."

He nodded, but scanned the apartment once more, his dark gaze flashing for a moment. "Well, goodnight then, Elle. I'll see you tomorrow."

"Goodnight, Thor." She fought the compulsion to curtsey.

He closed the door, and silence shrouded her. She stared at the door for several minutes, not moving, waiting. Waiting for someone to jump out. Waiting... for a sound of someone in metal armor. The smell of brimstone and coal. Something. Anything. But nothing came. Nothing jumped. Nothing emerged.

Without thinking, she raced straight to the door and locked both locks before running to her bedroom and throwing herself under the royal blue covers without even taking off her shoes.

She squeezed her eyes shut and pulled the covers over her head.

She was safe. She was safe. No one knew who she was. She was just being paranoid.

She thought of going to find Val, but if she did, Val would become even more overprotective.

She kicked off her shoes but didn't get out of bed. She blew out a breath and focused her thoughts on the one thing that actually made her feel safe.

Thor Odinson's face.

CHAPTER NINE

Elle inspected herself in the mirror and fiddled with her blouse. Emerald turned out to be a nice color on her. Back on Muspelheim, everything had been tainted by the yellowish-orange hues. But Midgard had no such problem, so she got to see the color clearly for the first time. She smoothed down her black slacks and slipped on her new ballet flats.

She sorted through the different items she'd bought at the drugstore. Various colors of powders, creams, and liquids meant to enhance her features, but she had no idea how to use them. Finally, she picked out a gold powder and dusted it over her eyelids and cheeks. Surprised by the glowy appearance it gave her, she decided to try the tube of light-peachy liquid. As she smoothed the sticky goo on her lips, she found herself, once again, pleased with the outcome, though her curls kept getting stuck in it.

A knock sounded on her door, making her jump. She looked at the clock. He was five minutes early, again. She appreciated that about him. On Muspelheim, all she'd done was wait. Another way for her father to remind her she was less important than well… anyone.

She slipped on her shoes and grabbed her coat. She smiled and opened the door.

Her face fell.

Val cocked an eyebrow at her and looked her up and down. "Going somewhere?"

Elle sighed. "To dinner."

Val leaned against the doorjamb. "Anyone I know?"

Elle rolled her eyes. They'd avoided talking all day during their shift. Val had seen her with Thor the night before, but had managed not to corner Elle about it until that moment.

"Have you told him?"

Elle bit her lip.

Val nodded. "So, he isn't aware your mother and I were kidnapped after Ragnarök and taken to Muspelheim as your father's prisoners. And you are the daughter of the beast who rained destruction down on his entire existence."

"Why are you trying to ruin this for me?"

Val's eyes softened. "I'm trying to protect you, like always. What do you think is going to happen when he finds out? Especially when he realizes that not only are you the daughter of Surtr, but also that you kept it from him."

"You told me not to tell him," she insisted.

"To keep you safe. But now…"

"What does it matter?" Elle yelled. "Everyone else knows."

Val's expression hardened. "But not everyone else wants your entire race wiped out."

Elle groaned. "Perhaps he won't care."

Val nodded. "If you truly believe that, then tell him. Tell him who you are."

Elle swallowed hard, and the stairs creaked as Thor's shaggy head appeared at the end of the hallway.

He stopped at the sight of her and smiled.

She smiled back.

"I should go," she said to Val.

Val nodded, and Elle shut the door behind herself. Val didn't move, so Elle walked around her and down the hall to Thor.

"Wow," he said. "And I didn't think you could be more stunning."

Elle's cheeks flushed. "You look great, too." And she meant it. He'd traded in his T-shirt for a black fitted button-up. Black slacks replaced his usual jeans and cut to his slim waist and rather sexy round rear. If she hadn't known better, she would have thought him a professional male model.

He held out his hand to her, and she took it, the familiar warmth traveling up her arm at his touch.

As they started down the stairs, Elle peeked over her shoulder to find Val hadn't moved as she watched them go.

"How did you bring this up to Midgard?" Elle asked.

"Through the portal," he said.

Thor chuckled, grabbed a helmet off the back of his bike, and strapped it to her head before putting on his own helmet. He tried not to stare at Elle in the beautiful green blouse that made her eyes shine, and her freckles stand out against her peachy skin. Her beautiful curls cascaded down her back, and he felt bad she had to put a helmet on. He should have thought of that. But… he'd never ridden one of his bikes with a female before.

Elle looked over the motorcycle. "Frigg let you bring it into the pub?"

"No, it was a different portal. A bigger one."

"A different portal?"

Thor studied her for a minute. "You're aware the one in the Raven Weaver isn't the only portal, right?"

She dropped her gaze.

"There are many portals in and out of Helheim."

"Can anyone come through?" Panic tinged her voice.

"No. There are Helborn guards. They know every soul and being in Helheim. They also know when someone hasn't obtained permission to be there, and they deal with them."

She nodded. "Wow. Hel thought of everything."

"Not really Hel."

"What do you mean?"

"Helheim is a part of the bigger realm that is the Underworld. Many deities of death have places there. But they are all overseen by Lucifer, the Midgardian version of Hel. He made the original realm. He granted Hel her portion to rule over. But even she has to answer to Lucifer."

"Who does he answer to?" she asked.

He chuckled. "That is up for debate. Come on. We have a reservation." He straddled his bike and motioned for her to sit behind him.

Elle slid over the bike. Thor grabbed her wrist and pulled her close against his back, pressing her hand into his stomach.

"Hang on to me," he said.

Her other arm snaked around his waist, and she clasped her hands together. He sucked in a breath at the warmth of her body against him. How long had it been since he'd been touched by a woman? Or better yet, wanted to be touched by one?

"Relax into me," he said, his voice raspy. "Let my body lead you."

She scooted closer, and her arms tightened around his waist as her body molded into his, and she set her chin on his back.

Thor turned over the engine and kicked the kickstand up. The bike rumbled beneath him, sending tiny vibrations up his thighs. The sensations mixed with her scent and the feel of her body against his made his chest squeeze. He remembered how she'd looked at him the night before. Like she'd wanted to kiss him or ask him to stay, but also something else. A tinge of fear had creased the corners of her eyes. So he hadn't done either. He'd simply left. Well, not truly. He'd spent fifteen minutes waiting at the top of the stairs to make sure she was okay and then another hour down in the bar with Heimdall before convincing himself that no one meant her harm. Then he had left.

Thor put on his blinker and pulled into traffic. Her entire body tensed around him like a form-fitting glove. The sensation made every nerve pay attention. Even the inconvenient parts of him.

Knock it off. It's not like a woman has never touched you before.

Thor rode down the street, and as they turned corners, Elle's body moved so easily with his, he couldn't tell where his body ended, and hers started. A feeling of oneness came over him, making Thor no longer want to go to dinner. As Thor leaned into a curve, the winding road beneath them seemed an endless ribbon of possibility. Elle's thighs pressed against his with a familiar warmth, her presence both a comfort and a sweet torment. Her scent- an intoxicating blend of something warm and spicy and flowers cut through the cool night air, making it hard for him to concentrate. He wanted to cruise to the coast highway and ride with her as far as they could go. Just the two of them. Away from everything and everyone else. Take her to a beach to watch the sunset and kiss her on the sand.

Elle's breath quickened as they turned another corner, leaning low to the ground. Her fingers shift, gripping him tighter and hooking her thumbs into his belt loops. The touch sent electricity skittering up his spine.

Thor exhaled sharply. A barrage of thoughts storms through him: Stop here. Hold onto this. Let this night unravel into passion.

Instead, he turned a corner and pulled up in front of a Japanese restaurant. He turned off the bike and put down the kickstand. He removed his helmet and realized Elle still hadn't released her grip on him. He patted her hands.

"You can let go now, we're here."

She lay her cheek on his shoulder, and he barely heard her whisper, "What if I don't want to?"

His gut clenched, and he wanted to tell her not to. Wanted to turn around and pull her lips to his. To kiss her on his bike, not caring who saw them. Screw dinner, they'd grab something on the road.

Again, Frigg's words floated back, and he sucked in a breath.

"We can do it again. After we eat."

Elle nodded and took off her helmet. "Deal."

Thor picked up a piece of salmon sashimi, topped it with ginger, dipped it in soy sauce, and held it out to Elle.

She wrinkled her nose. "I thought I said no raw fish."

"No, you said you didn't want raw fish last night. Tonight is a different night."

She eyed him skeptically.

"Try it."

She scrunched up her face, leaned forward, and opened her mouth. Thor placed the fish on her tongue, and she began to chew. At first, her expression remained confused, but confusion turned to revulsion. She grabbed her napkin and spit into it before chugging down half a cup of soda.

"No. No. Nope." She waved her hands at him. "That is awful. Not tonight either. Not any night to be clear."

"It's delicious," Thor retorted. "You have to give it a chance."

"I did give it a chance, and the answer is no. It's slimy and chewy and... orange."

Thor laughed. "Orange? You don't like it because it's orange?"

"No. I don't like it because it's raw fish." She wiped her tongue on her napkin. "I'm beginning to think you are trying to starve me, Thor Odinson. First, no dinner last night, and now this."

"I offered to take you out to eat last night."

"You did. But if it had been anything like this, I would have been in the same spot, starving."

"All right. All right." Thor motioned the waitress over. "Please bring the lady a bento box with chicken teriyaki."

"Is the chicken raw?"

"No," said Thor. "It's cooked."

Elle smiled. "That I will eat."

"Tell me about yourself," Elle said.

"I thought you knew everything about me already." He laughed.

"Clearly, I don't. The books say nothing of sushi or motorcycles. I read what books say. I heard what people say. But I don't know what you say."

Thor looked at her for a moment. "Well, I come from a massive, dysfunctional, semi-intermarried family. I have five brothers, not including the ones my parents don't talk about. I grew up on Asgard. I was taught to fight. I fought. I fought more. Then it ended."

She studied him as he piled ginger and green paste on his pieces of fish before dipping them in soy sauce and popping them into his mouth. She saw his pain. His loneliness. She wondered for a moment what he had been like before Ragnarök. She assumed he would have been louder, more boisterous. Regaling people with his tales and wooing women to his bed.

"What are you thinking?"

She sipped her soda. "I wondered why you chose to stay in Helheim when you could live up here."

"Midgard is chaos. Down there is not. Humans are unpredictable, violent, and in some ways primitive. Helheim is organized. It has a hierarchy, and no matter what happens, hierarchy doesn't change. If you step out of line, you are punished. If you obey the laws, no one bothers you."

"I would have thought you'd prefer to be on Midgard, helping, trying to make order of the chaos."

"There is no making order of this place. Many have tried and failed. Until they unite and see themselves as equals and one people, there will never be peace. So, there's nothing I can do for them."

She'd never thought about that before. But then she hadn't been in Midgard long. Yet, she couldn't help but feel that the Asgardians could help Midgard so much. Especially the paranormal community. The werewolves and vampires, fae and demons, and every other race.

"Interesting," she finally said.

"Do you think I'm wrong?"

"I am in no position to tell anyone what they should do with their life."

"Have you thought about what you want to do with your life? I'm sure you don't want to waitress at the Raven Weaver for the rest of your existence."

"Lady Frigg has been kind to me, but no, I do not wish to waitress forever."

"Have you found anything else you might want to do?"

Elle's food arrived in a small box. Chicken in a brown sauce, a salad, some dumplings, and rice. She stabbed at her salad. She'd spent a lot of time thinking about what to do with the rest of her life now that she had a choice as well as time to herself.

"I'm not sure," she finally said. "I love to read, and I've always loved music, but I haven't researched what I could do with either. I've seen the people doing karaoke at the Raven Weaver, and not only do I not understand why they do it, but I don't think I'd ever sing in front of people."

"You can sing?"

Elle shrugged. "Yes. I've never sung in front of other people, though."

"Would you sing for me?"

She stared at him for a moment. "Now?"

He squeezed her hand. "When you're comfortable."

Her stomach twisted like her insides had turned to worms. "All right."

He smiled at her, making her smile in return.

"What about jewelry making?" he asked. "Have you ever worked with anything more than base metal?"

"I've polished rocks before."

"Polished rocks?"

"Yeah. I found different rocks around... where I lived, and if I liked their color, I would pick them up and polish them until they were the shape and size I liked."

He stared at her. "By hand?"

She nodded.

"How long did that take?"

"A couple of them took me several years."

He shook his head. "You are indeed incredibly talented, as well as patient. I could never be that patient."

"I am sure if you'd had as much time on your hands as I used to, you'd learn to become that patient."

Thor snorted. "I lived in Valhalla, where I had nothing but time, and I'm still impatient."

She laughed. "Maybe that's a 'you' problem."

"I'm sure it is. Even though I enjoy taking motorcycles apart and putting them back together, I find myself getting halfway through and suddenly wishing I was already done."

THEY FINISHED THE REST OF THEIR MEAL TALKING ABOUT THINGS TO do in Los Angeles and the parts of Midgard Thor had visited in the past century. The conversation flowed easily, as if they'd been friends for years.

She learned Thor had traveled extensively when he'd first arrived. He'd taken to riding a motorcycle around the whole country of America before settling down in Helheim. Surprisingly, his bikes were in demand, and he made a decent living. Not that he needed money.

"Have you thought about moving to Helheim?" asked Thor as they finished up.

"To be honest, it scares me."

"Has anything ever happened when there?"

The memories from their walk to the Raven Weaver floated back. "No, it's just so dark and ominous."

"But it's also peaceful. Usually quiet, at least in my neck of the woods. And I find the Helmarked who live there to be decent. They want to live well, have fun, and be happy."

"Isn't that what mortals want?"

"Yes, but the difference is, unlike in Helheim, mortals are in such a rush to have everything now. But when you live as long as we do, you learn a bit of patience or at least become accustomed to waiting."

"But you said you're impatient."

"I am. But I'm a thousand times more patient than I used to be."

She chuckled. "Wow. I can't imagine."

Thor pulled out some money and tossed it on the table. "Are you ready to go back?"

"Are you?" She wasn't ready to end the night, but she didn't want to keep him longer than he wanted.

"If you aren't too tired, I'd like to show you one more place."

"Does it involve more fish?"

Thor laughed. "The next place will make up for the raw fish. Promise."

She nodded. “Okay. You have one more chance to get me to trust you.”

“Then I'd better not disappoint.”

CHAPTER TEN

"The Odyssey?"

"Don't judge this place by the outside, trust me, you are going to love it."

Thor led her to the deep blue door and pulled it open. It squeaked loudly, breaking the silence from within. The shop smelled of old paper and binding glue, layered over coffee that had gone cold hours ago. Somewhere deeper in the stacks, a kettle whistled and cut off. It had been a while since he'd been there, and it was obvious the place had gotten busier since his last venture inside.

He took Elle's hand and led her through a crowded aisle of shelves lined with books. He steered her away from a pile teetering on the floor and had to actually push a cart out of the way to reach the front desk. The cart's wheels shrieked against the floorboards. Books were stacked everywhere. On the counter, under the counter, in towers along the baseboards that leaned like drunk sentries.

A landslide of paperbacks buried the front desk. Their cracked spines showed titles in half a dozen genres. Atop the stack, a brass bell sat, green with tarnish.

He stood for a moment on the hard wooden floor and placed Elle in the center of the shop. Elle's mouth dropped open as she turned in a circle.

"What is this place?" she asked.

"A used bookstore."

The words echoed off close walls. The narrow but deep shop stretched back into shadow, where more shelves crowded together like teeth. Burgundy rugs, threadbare at the paths, covered the wooden floor between aisles. Hand-lettered signs in chalk hung from the shelf ends- POETRY, HISTORY, ROMANCE. A tabby cat was curled on a stack of atlases near the window, its tail draped over a globe the color of old tea.

Elle looked upward, and Thor followed her gaze to where the tops of the shelves reached the ceiling.

"Don't worry, they have rolling ladders if you want to climb up. I thought about taking you to a regular bookstore, but why waste money when I could bring you here? The books here are a fraction of the price of new ones."

Elle's eyes sparkled. "That means I can buy substantially more books."

Thor scratched his head. "Well, that's not exactly what I was going for, but I guess it's true. Does this mean you trust me again after the sushi debacle?"

“Definitely.” Elle squealed with delight and kissed him on the cheek before running to the nearest aisle and starting at the bottom, scanning the books. She pulled one off the shelf and flipped through the pages while inhaling.

"Oh boy." Thor sighed. Maybe he should have brought her on her day off.

After following Elle for close to an hour, with his arms full of books, Thor walked to the lounge area and set the books on a table while he dropped into a plush, cobalt velvet chair. He sat for a moment, trying to calculate how long it would take Elle to go through the whole store. At the rate she was moving, they might be done by his three thousandth birthday. But then she would want to start over because there would be so many new books.

Thor smiled, glad he'd done something for her that she truly loved. It did bum him out about sushi, though. He'd have to take her to Chinese food next time.

He scanned the stack of books Elle had picked. They were all nonfiction books about gems, jewelry-making, and geology.

Elle walked up beaming, arms full of another stack of books. "I've finished the first row."

"Did you leave books for anyone else?"

Elle's eyes narrowed. "Ha-ha."

She set the second stack next to the first and began looking through them.

Thor picked up a book. "Do you really want all these?"

She shrugged. "I want to read them. I'm not sure I want to keep them all, but learning about geology, rocks, and metals on Midgard is fascinating."

"Why buy them if you aren't going to keep them all?"

Her brow knit. "I'm not going to steal them."

Thor shook his head. "I should have taken you to the public library."

"Public library?"

"A place where you can borrow books for free, and when you are done reading them, you return them."

Elle's eyes widened so far he thought they might pop out. "Is... is anyone allowed to borrow the books?" she whispered.

"As long as you have a library card."

Elle stared at him as if trying to comprehend the idea.

"Can we go there next?"

"Sadly, they're closing soon. We need your ID as well. Loki gave you papers, I assume."

She nodded.

"Well, we'll need those. Then you go in, fill out a form, and they give you a library card, and you're all set."

Elle continued to sit, unblinkingly, as if envisioning all the books.

"For free," she mused.

Thor chuckled. "Okay, okay, don't hurt your brain. Why don't you pick out a few books to tide you over until we can go on your next day off?"

Elle nodded and thumbed through the stacks of books. She separated them into three piles and picked up the largest, of about fifteen books. "I'm ready."

"Is your next day off in six months?" he chided.

"I haven't taken a day off since I got here. I'm not sure how often I have them."

"Once or twice a week."

Her eyebrows raised. "Two days a week? To... do what I want?"

"You could work even less if you wanted."

She shook her head. "I need to be of service. I need to repay Lady Frigg."

"You realize Frigg doesn't expect repayment, right?"

"I want to make sure I do my part. That I work hard, and she is pleased."

Thor reached out and took Elle's hand. "Elle, Frigg won't send you away if you make a mistake or want something for yourself."

Elle wouldn't meet his eye.

"Elle, look at me."

She lifted her gaze.

"Elle, no one is going to send you back where you came from. No one is going to get mad at you and tell whoever you are hiding from where you are."

She didn't speak for a moment. "I... I just..."

So, he was right. She was running from someone.

Thor squeezed her hand. "Elle, I understand you are scared of something, someone, but my family adores you. Frigg and Loki wouldn't have helped you, only to sell you out. You are one of us now. We will protect you like we would each other."

Her chin quavered, and she nodded.

Thor touched her cheek, and she smiled at him. Every particle of his body meant what he'd said. Though he'd not known her long, Thor was certain of one thing. He would never let anyone hurt Elle again. No matter what he had to do to protect her.

THOR HELPED ELLE CARRY HER CHOSEN BOOKS INTO HER FLAT.

"You can put them on the table," she said, setting her jacket down. She glanced around to make sure she'd cleaned her place, but like always, it remained spotless.

Thor set the stack of books on the coffee table. "I like what you've done with the place."

"What do you mean?"

"The neutral colors make the place appear bigger. I like it."

"Oh... thank you. Most of the things I got at a thrift store."

Thor headed to her bookshelf and picked up one of the figurines Val made her.

"Did you make these?"

"No, Val did. She made them for me when I was young, so I'd have something to play with. Probably to grab a small break from having to read to me."

Thor smiled and put it back. He picked up one of her rocks.

"Is this one of your polished rocks?"

"Yes. That is one of the ones which took me a year to complete."

He stared at it for a moment. "You know what this is, right?"

"A sparkly red rock?"

He chuckled. "It's a ruby. They are rare on Midgard. People pay a lot of money for them."

"Do they?"

He held the stone up to the light. "One of this size would net you several thousand dollars."

"What?" She couldn't believe it. The red rocks had been all over Muspelheim.

He nodded. "How did you learn to put all these facets in it?"

"Facets?"

"Yeah, the angles you carved in to be able to refract the light so it looks... glitterier."

"Oh... I saw someone wearing one that looked like it once and I... did it."

He stared at her in astonishment. "You should come back to my shop and work with the tools I have."

She nodded. "I'd love to. Thank you."

Thor put the stone back and checked out the other items and books on her shelf. Elle held her breath, afraid he might find something he would recognize as being from Muspelheim, but after a minute, he turned to her.

"I should let you go so you can sleep."

"Of course." She tried to keep disappointment out of her voice. She wasn't ready for Thor to leave yet.

Thor loomed closer, his presence a magnetic force that pulled Elle into his orbit. His steps faltered for a heartbeat, the tension in his jaw giving way to a soft sigh before he enveloped her in his embrace. The warmth radiating from him intoxicating, and Elle found herself sinking into it, her breath hitching as she rested against the solid expanse of his chest.

Her hand fluttered at the small of his back, caught between the desire to clutch onto him and the need to maintain composure. The air around them charged, carrying the scent of ozone and iron- a testament to his power and stability.

Time stretched as they stood entwined. And her magic swirled deep inside her, but not out of fear, out of something else.

Finally, Thor pushed away. His gaze landed on her face and lifted his hand to cup her cheek. "What is it about you?"

Her chest constricted. "What... what do you mean?"

"I don't know. I just... I don't want to leave because when I do, I can't get you out of my head. I want to protect you, kiss you, and take care of you. You're like a sweet bird who is so fragile yet so strong at the same time. I can't put my finger on it. I just... want to make sure no one ever hurts you again."

Elle couldn't help the tears that welled in her eyes. No one had ever spoken so kindly to her before. No one had ever said anything remotely close to telling her they wanted to take care of her. Val, though her best friend, wasn't tender. Her way of showing Elle she loved her was to teach her to fight and to help her become as strong as possible. Hugs and laughs weren't something they shared.

Thor brushed a tear from her eye with the pad of his thumb, and her body flushed. He leaned in and kissed the trail the tear had taken up her cheek. Then he kissed across her forehead and down her nose to her lips.

The taste of him made her moan. Embarrassed, she began to pull away, yet his hand rested at the nape of her neck, holding her in place with an unspoken command. Desire pooled in her belly. Heat and need blossomed inside her, and when his lips parted, she let his tongue entwine with hers.

Sensations rushed through her, and kissing him wasn't enough. She wanted his hands on her skin. Wanted him naked and to run her hands down the planes of his body.

Her breath hitched as his palms glided down her spine, pausing with deliberate intent before claiming the curve of her rear. She stiffened, and his grip softened, fingers trembling as if waging a silent battle for control.

Their lips parted, leaving the air charged between them. Thor's gaze met hers- steady and piercing- before he looked away, swallowing hard.

His husky whisper echoed in the space around them. "Say the word, and I'll stop."

Her heart hammered in her chest like a drum. She could hardly think, but she didn't want him to stop.

Tingles raced over her skin. All the stories she'd read about in her father's library burst into her mind, and she wanted to feel what it was like to make love to someone. But not someone, Thor, God of Thunder.

THOR CRADLED ELLE IN HIS ARMS. TASTING HER SWEET LIPS WHILE her body warmed him from the inside out was almost more than he could take. He wanted more than to make love to her. He wanted her like he'd never wanted another.

Sweet and tender, innocent and kind, she was more than a one-night stand; she was someone he could spend the rest of his immortal days with. Someone he would never tire of. Someone who would bring peace into his chaotic world. Someone to share himself with, someone... to grow older with.

When she didn't tell him to stop, he kissed her harder. How was it possible he'd found her, and she'd woven her way into his heart so fast? In his thousands and thousands of years of life, he'd never let anyone in so fast.

She pressed her soft, willowy body into his and met his kisses with equal fervor. He lifted her into his arms and carried her to the bed in the corner. She stared at him, her eyes hooded with desire as he led her to her bedroom, lay her on the bed, and stripped off his jacket.

He lay atop her and relished her soft curves pressing against his chest and hipbones.

She pulled his mouth back to hers and kissed him fiercely, making his desire for her spike further. So timid and yet so willful.

He ran his fingers under the hem of her shirt, and she made a mewling sound that almost undid him. He needed to keep control. He couldn't rush her. He wanted to relish her, memorize her. Give her everything she'd ever wanted, but stop in an instant if she told him to.

It had never been that way for him before. He'd never wanted to give without taking. Never gone gentle or slow. But with Elle, he wanted to savor every second.

He trailed his palm over her soft belly and down between her thighs. He parted her legs so he could settle between them. His erection pushed against his pants and rested against her core.

She sucked in a sharp breath and arched toward him. Thor ran his hand up over her shirt and cupped her small breast through the fabric. She moaned and ran her hands under the back of his shirt. Her soft fingers traced his skin, making parts of him wake up for the first time in a long time and take notice.

Thor kissed down her throat to her collarbone. He kissed across it and then down to her other breast. He nipped at it through the fabric and continued lower and kissed down her side. She gripped his shirt, and the further he slid, the higher it rose until she had lifted it off him. He tossed it to the ground and then lifted the edge of her T-shirt and kissed across her flat stomach. She dug her nails into his shoulders, hitting one of his various scars and making a jolt of pain shoot up his neck, the pain mixing with his pleasure in a deliciously impossible way.

He kissed his way up her torso to her breasts. He slid her shirt up, and she pulled it off as he unclasped her pink lacy bra and slid it off her shoulders. He gazed upon her in the moonlight, and she flushed with a peachy glow and looked away.

"Look at me," he commanded.

Her gaze traveled back to his.

"Don't you know how utterly gorgeous you are?"

"It's... it's not that..."

"What is it?" He searched her face, and realization dawned. "You've never done this before."

She shook her head.

Shit. That wasn't something he expected.

"Elle, is this something you want to do?"

"Yes. Gods yes. But... I... I need to tell you something."

He kissed her. "You don't need to tell me anything. I've tried to force you to tell me about your past, but I don't care."

"You don't?"

"I mean, I do. But only if you want to tell me. I don't want you to do anything you aren't comfortable with. Whether it be talking about your past or this. If you aren't ready, I understand. I need you to believe me when I tell you I am not interested in simply having sex with you. When I look at you, I see... forever." Thor felt ridiculous saying the words he held in his heart, but somehow, he couldn't stop himself. He needed her to believe that his intentions were nothing but sincere.

Without a word, she pulled his mouth back to hers and ran her hands down his torso to his belt buckle, which he whipped off before unzipping his pants.

Elle had no idea what she was doing. It was like her body had complete control of her, and she was a passenger along for the ride. She fumbled with his buckle with shaky hands as he kissed down the side of her neck and over her breasts, making them pucker with sensitivity. Her hands stopped moving as the pure bliss of his mouth on her skin invaded every inch of her.

He waited, his eyes questioning.

"Don't stop," she breathed.

Thor undid the buckle to his belt and unbuttoned his jeans. She peeked down to see he wore nothing underneath. How could that be comfortable?

She didn't have time to think about it as he kissed down her stomach, stopped at her waistband, and hooked his fingers underneath. She stiffened, and Thor didn't do more than trace his fingers under the waistband of her leggings. He raised up and kissed her again, his mouth hot and greedy. His own need only fed into hers, making her heat further.

Slowly, he slid his palm down her leggings between her legs. The sensation jolted through her, and she arched against him and grabbed his shoulders, her nails digging into his skin. Somehow, the motion made his kisses deeper and harder.

She ran her fingers down his back and grabbed his rear. Firm and round, it showed not an ounce of fat on it. She gripped his rear and pulled his hips toward her. His length ground into her most sensitive area, and she melted. Every inch of her buzzed with electricity. She wanted him. Needed him.

Elle slid her hand between them and cupped his length. Thor groaned against her mouth and bit her lip before dropping his head to her shoulder and breathing hard.

He nipped her neck while she used her fingers to stroke the length of him. His soft skin molded to her fingers, and she soon found herself pushing his jeans down farther.

"Thor..." she whispered. "I want you."

He didn't have to be told a second time. He slid off the bed, and his boots and pants hit the floor with a clunk.

Elle took in the length of his taut, muscular body and understood why he was a god. He'd been chiseled like nothing she had ever seen. And the scars he wore attested to his accomplishments. All tanned skin and firmly cut muscles. He sported a small light trail of hair down his belly that made her want to feel its silky fibers between her fingers.

Thor crawled back up on the bed and skimmed his fingers under the edge of her leggings again, and this time he slipped them as well as her panties down her legs and threw them to the ground.

He took her in for a moment as if committing every inch of her to memory. Then, starting at her toes, he bent down and pressed a kiss into her foot. Her ankle. Her calf. Behind her knee. And up the inside of her thigh. Her core clenched as his warm breath hit her straight between her legs.

She tangled her fingers in his thick hair as he hooked his arms around her thighs and pulled her into his face.

Nervousness and embarrassment flooded her. What would Val think if she saw Elle like this? Giving in to Thor's touch so easily. But more than that, she worried what Thor thought. Thought of her body, her scent, her touch. But every worry fled as he licked up her most sensitive area, making her hips buck. She'd never known anything could feel so amazing.

Thor stroked her with his tongue, making her body spasm and tremble. Something wound tight inside her, and then slowly his finger entered her. The sensation almost had Elle shoot off the bed. She grabbed Thor's head harder as he kissed the inside of her thigh and used his fingers to bring her unfathomable pleasure.

Everything she'd ever read or seen amongst her father's men in the castle had been nothing like that. They'd taken women from behind. Forcefully. She'd never known such pleasure was possible for a woman. Val had told her on her wedding night, she was to lie still and let Thadren do what he needed to.

But what Thor seemed to need to do... She was perfectly fine letting him.

Shivers and tingles raced through her body and up her thighs to her core. Her body wound tight, looking for something. Something higher, stronger.

Thor rose up, and she yanked his mouth to hers. She needed him. Wanted every inch of his body on hers and wanted him inside her.

She reached down and gripped him tight once more, guiding him toward her core. He broke the kiss for a moment.

"Easy," he said. "I don't want to hurt you."

"You won't," she said, not sounding as sure.

"Slow," said Thor.

He circled a finger around her entrance again, and then the pressure of his length rested in the same place. He bit her lip, catching her attention, and slowed his kisses, letting his tongue play with hers.

She went to reach for him again, but he pinned her hands above her head.

"Trust me," he said, before bowing his head and sucking one of her breasts into his mouth.

Elle thought she might burst from desire as Thor circled his hips against hers and slowly, infinitesimally, he pressed into her. At first, her body resisted.

“Relax. I won’t hurt you,” he promised. “And if you want me to stop-”

"No," she breathed. "Don't stop."

He kissed her again, pushing against her and then withdrawing. Deeper, and then withdrawing again. Then deeper still before pulling back.

She wanted to scream at him. To grab his hips and force him fully inside her, but he held her wrists over her head and continued kissing her.

He pushed inside her, and there was a moment of resistance before pressure, and then he filled her. The sensation both thrilled and terrified her. Thor groaned and sucked in a sharp breath. He continued to kiss her, allowing her a moment to process. But the moment morphed into need. She needed him. Wanted to make love to him, not lie there and do nothing.

Elle tried to move her hips back and forth. Thor's kisses grew hungrier, and then she wasn't the only one moving. Thor drew out sensations in her body she'd never experienced. Soon, the friction between them grew, and the rhythmical lovemaking became faster and less gentle. Her body spiraled deeper and deeper.

He called her name, letting go of one of her hands to grip her hip and pull her closer. His body rolled down on her, hitting a part of her she didn't know existed. Suddenly, something burst inside her. Body clenching, muscles tight, the greatest pleasure she had experienced slammed through her.

She fought to hang on to Thor as his movements became frenzied and he released her second hand to grab the headboard of her bed.

Elle lifted his chin and made him look at her as his body shuddered, and he called her name. Outside, lightning crackled, and thunder rolled through the sky like a thousand stampeding stallions. Every inch of him tensed, and she continued to pull his hips against hers as his face twisted in a mix of agony and ecstasy. Eventually, he collapsed on top of her. He breathed heavy, and his heartbeat pounded against hers. Then he lifted himself up on his elbows and kissed her again. Tenderly, like he was afraid he'd hurt her.

She cupped his face in her hands, and lightning flashed in his eyes.

"Elle..."

"Thor."

He kissed her again before rolling off her and pulling her into his arms.

His body wrapped around hers, making her tingle from head to toe. Thor, God of Thunder, had made love to her. Sutrelle-daughter of his enemy.

Elle squeezed her eyes shut, a tremor running through her body that had nothing to do with pleasure. The weight of her deception pressed against her chest, making each breath shallow and painful. Thor's arms around her felt like a sanctuary and a trap. His heartbeat thrummed against her back, strong and steady, while hers raced with panic.

"Are you all right?" Thor's voice rumbled against her ear, his breath warm on her neck.

She nodded, not trusting her voice. How did she tell him now? The words stuck in her throat like shards of glass. *Surtr's daughter. Enemy of Asgard. Liar.*

"Elle?" His fingers traced gentle patterns along her arm, raising goosebumps in their wake. "You're shaking."

She rolled to face him, forcing herself to open her eyes. His face was so close, blue eyes still glinting with remnants of lightning, stubble rough against her palm as she touched his cheek. The tenderness in his gaze made something crack inside her.

"I'm just..." The lie died on her lips. She couldn't bear to add another falsehood to the mountain between them. Not now. Not after what they'd shared.

Thor brushed a strand of hair from her face, his calloused thumb lingering at her temple. "Whatever it is, you can tell me."

A sob built in her throat. The secret she carried was a living thing, clawing to get out. If she told him, she would lose him. If she didn't, she would lose herself.

"I'm afraid," she whispered.

His brow furrowed, protective instinct flashing across his features. "Of what?"

"That this isn't real." It wasn't what she meant to say, but it wasn't untrue. "That when you know me- truly know me- you'll..."

"I'll what?" His voice was gentle, but his body tensed.

Elle pressed her forehead against his chest, breathing in his scent- ozone and iron and something uniquely him. Her heart lay raw, exposed, like an open wound. She had never given herself to anyone before- not her body, not her trust, not her heart. Now she had surrendered all three, and the vulnerability terrified her.

"You won't like me," she whispered into his skin. "Or worse… You won't want me anymore."

Thor's arms tightened around her. "Elle, look at me."

She couldn't. If she did, she might shatter.

His fingers tilted her chin up, forcing her gaze to meet his. "Nothing you tell me would make that happen."

A tear slipped down her cheek. "You don't know that."

"I know you." His thumb caught the tear. "I may not know where you came from or what you're running from, but I know who you are. Here." He placed his hand over her heart. "And that's what matters to me. You are what matters to me."

CHAPTER ELEVEN

A twitch awoke Elle. She opened her eyes, and Thor twitched again. She looked at his still-sleeping face, twisted in anger. For a moment, he didn't move, and then he shouted and swung wildly. Elle scrambled out of the way.

"Thor?"

He struck out again, rolled over, and fell out of the bed, hitting the floor with a thump.

"Thor!" Elle ran around the bed.

Thor jumped to his feet, his body in a tense, defensive stance. He peered at her through the darkness like he couldn't place her.

"Thor, it's... It's Elle. Remember?"

He said her name uncertainly and blinked several times before relaxing. "Elle. I'm... I'm so sorry."

"Are you okay?" She took a tentative step toward him but stopped.

He stood for a minute gathering himself, blew out a long breath, and sat on the edge of the bed. She waited before sitting next to him.

He hung his head in his hands. She wanted to reach out to him but wasn't sure he wanted her to.

Finally, he looked at her. "I didn't hurt you, did I?"

"No. Are you okay, though?"

He hung his head again. "It's been thousands of years, and still I suffer from nightmares."

"Of what?"

"Everything. The wars. The executions. The fighting. Just... all of it."

"But you're a hero."

He snorted. "Like they said, I ate my goats all the time?"

"You don't see yourself as a hero?"

"I did what I had to do to save my people and my family. But in the end... it was all destroyed anyway."

Elle's stomach squeezed. "Ragnarök."

Thor nodded. "No matter what I did. No matter how many realms I took. No matter how many battles I won, in the end, we lost everything anyway."

"But that was so long ago. Now you've made a new home for yourself and your family."

"But the remaining Asgardians were displaced. Many died. Some ended up here. Others in other realms. But it's not the same."

"Your people are in Valhalla. Paradise. Being cared for by virgins, fed meat and ale until they are content every day."

"In theory, that sounds wonderful, but after a thousand years or more, you start to go stir crazy. At least I did. The peace felt... fake. Forced. In the end, my family and I couldn't handle it."

"So that's why you all went to Helheim."

He nodded. "It was my father's idea, and to be honest, I've never seen him happier. I've never seen anyone in my family happier. Even in Valhalla, we were forced to mitigate any problems. But here. Here we are only responsible for ourselves. It's the first time I've been free to be myself in my entire life."

"That's a good thing then, right?" She smiled at him. "Maybe Ragnarök was a blessing."

He stared at her for a moment. "Why did you come to Midgard?"

Elle chewed the inside of her lip. "My... father wanted me to marry a man not of my choosing."

"Why didn't you say no?"

She chuckled, humorlessly. "Where I come from, women don't say no."

"So, you ran?"

She nodded.

"Do you miss it?"

"No," she said too quickly. "I mean... back home, I wasn't allowed to do anything, but here, like you, I am finally free to do what I want. If I want to eat, I eat. If I want to sleep, I sleep. No one tells me when or what to do. No one hits me for looking them in the eye. No one grabs me for voicing my opinion. No one kicks at me to watch me flinch, so they can laugh."

Thor stared at her with those flashing lightning eyes. "Tell me where you are from, and I will again become the hero people once thought I was, and I'll kill them all for daring to breathe the same air you used to."

She didn't need to ask if he jested. The ice in his voice and in his eyes said he meant it.

Elle swallowed hard. "Thank you, but no. I like who you are

now. I'd hate to add to the nightmares by making you do something no longer in your nature."

Thor raised his hand and cupped her cheek. "You are too good for me, Elle. I don't deserve you."

She pulled from his reach. "Don't say that. It isn't true. You don't know me. You don't know who I really am."

He pulled her face back to his. "I know everything I need to. As you said, I'm not the person I used to be. I don't care where you came from. I don't care who you used to be. I'll never let anyone hurt you again, if you'll let me."

Elle's heart fluttered. How had it happened? How had she gotten so attached to him in such a short amount of time? She didn't care. In that moment, she wanted nothing more than to lie in Thor's muscular protective arms for the rest of her life.

"I think I'd like that."

Thor pulled her into his arms, and they lay back on the bed. She squeezed her eyes shut and took a deep breath before beginning to sing. Thor's breathing stilled for a moment, and she laid her hand on his chest and continued. His warm hands roamed her body, and as soon as she finished her song, his lips found hers again.

"Elle, you become more beautiful to me with every passing second."

He kissed her hard.

They made love several more times before falling back to sleep as the sun began to rise.

THOR AWAKENED TO A KNOCK ON THE DOOR. HE ROLLED OVER TO find Elle already dressed in her uniform, shoes in hand. She walked to the door and opened it a crack.

She spoke in hushed tones to someone on the other side, then closed the door. After a minute, she turned back and spotted him.

"I'm sorry," she said. "I tried not to wake you. You didn't sleep well, and I wanted you to be able to sleep in."

"To be honest, I don't sleep much. To me, this is sleeping in."

She gave him a quizzical expression. "How sad. One of the things I've loved the most since I've been here is sleeping."

He chuckled. "When you're as old as I am, you will find sleep to be more necessity, less luxury."

"Well, for now, I'll take my luxuries where I can." She smiled and sat at the table to put on her shoes.

"You headed to work?"

She nodded. "Not as long as yesterday, but I do have a six-hour shift."

He didn't like the idea of her working around the rowdy Midgardians. He wanted to tell her to stop and let him take care of her. But she needed to stand on her own two feet. Needed to learn to be her own person, and he couldn't selfishly take that from her because he wanted to protect her.

"You're gonna be off in time to go to my dad's family dinner, right?"

She stopped tying her shoes. "Are you sure you want me there? I mean, it is a family thing."

"Of course, I want you there. If for nothing else, then to distract my family from pestering me with questions about how I'm doing."

Her lips twisted into a wry smile. "Oh, so you're using me as a diversion?"

"My father, brothers, and cousins were never able to resist a pretty face."

She cocked an eyebrow. "What about you?"

Thor smiled. "Luckily, I have you, and I don't have to resist."

She chuckled and crossed to the bed. He swung his legs over the edge and pulled her to him. The scent of her clean hair enveloped him as he kissed her. He didn't want her to go. Didn't want her away from him. Wanted to take her down to his place and keep her there forever by his side.

He kissed her, and she raked her hands through his long hair and leaned into him. A sharp knock sounded on the door, and she groaned and broke away.

"I need to go."

"Stay." He couldn't hold the plea from his voice.

Her brow creased, and she bit her lip.

No. That wasn't right. She needed her independence. He had to let her have it.

"It's okay, Beautiful. You go to work, I'll see you tonight."

"Are you sure?"

He nodded and then kissed her again. "I don't want to make you late."

She smiled. "You would be worth it."

THOR SPENT THE DAY WORKING ON HIS DAD'S BIKE. TIME FLEW, AND before he realized it, it was time to pick up Elle. He'd not looked forward to something in so long that the sensation left him anxious.

Anxious? He'd never been anxious. Not before battle, not before ceremonies, not before anything. But somehow introducing Elle to his family made him anxious. Not because he was afraid they wouldn't like her, how could they not? But because he was afraid they would do something to scare her off. And he would do anything, go anywhere to keep her. Even if it meant leaving his family.

Thor walked through the portal to Midgard and jogged up the stairs. Heimdall nodded to him as Thor headed to the lofts. When he got to Elle's door, he found it open.

"I'm telling you, this isn't a good idea," said someone.

"Why?" Elle asked. "Thor and his entire family will be there."

"Exactly."

"I can't be safer anywhere in Helheim than with the entire family of Norse gods."

"That's not what I mean."

"I can't be afraid forever, Val. You brought me here to have a life. That's what I'm doing. Would you rather I fell for a Helborn or something else?"

"Of course not, it's just-"

"What? You're going too."

Thor knocked on the door, and it swung inward. Val turned to him. Both she and Elle wore beautiful, expensive dresses and heels. Elle's red hair had been pulled off her neck, and her crimson dress showed off her flawless peachy skin. It hung off her shoulders and swathed her curves in satiny sumptuousness.

Maybe they could skip the family dinner. He wasn't totally sure he wanted his brothers to see her looking like that. It had been a long time since he'd had to fight his brothers; it would be a shame to have to hurt one of them tonight to keep them off her.

Val eyed him for a moment and then strode from the room, stomped down the hall, and disappeared down the stairs.

"She doesn't like me," Thor said. "I'm not used to that."

"Don't take it too hard. She doesn't like anyone."

He wondered what made her angry. Had she been through the same things Elle had?

"Are you ready?" Elle asked.

Thor nodded.

She walked to the door, and he bent in and kissed her cheek. "You look amazing."

She smiled. "Thank you. I wasn't sure if it was too much."

"Not for me," Thor said. "I hope I can keep myself from peeling the dress off you until we are alone."

Elle blushed, and he took her hand.

"I'm going to warn you, if my brothers hit on you, I may hurt them."

She frowned. "I don't want to cause issues between you and your family."

He leaned in and kissed her. "You're worth it. Maybe I should take the goats with us. They'll be sure no one bothers you."

She chuckled. "Even you."

"True. No goats then."

She nodded.

"I want to prepare you," he said as they walked down the stairs. "My dad's place can be... a bit... much, if you haven't been before."

"What do you mean?"

Thor scratched his head. "It's a gentlemen's club. It caters to men."

"And?"

"There are women dancers, and not all wear clothes."

Elle's eyes widened. "Oh."

"There's nothing bad going on. He doesn't allow prostitution or anything, but he likes pretty women, and he's always had a thing for burlesque shows."

"Burlesque?"

"It's like a stage show. A play, kind of. With singing, and dancing, and the women aren't always fully clothed."

"Oh."

Suddenly, Thor didn't want to take Elle to Valhalla's Throne anymore. Someone of her delicate sensibilities shouldn't be forced to witness things like that.

"We don't have to go," he said. "I'm fine not going."

"No," she said quickly. "I want to."

He cocked an eyebrow at her and pulled her through the portal.

"I don't mean like that," she said. "I've seen enough naked women in my lifetime. I want to go because it's your family."

They walked toward the exit of the Raven Weaver with all eyes upon them. "Are you sure, because I'm still open to taking you to my second favorite restaurant instead."

"I'll take naked ladies over raw fish any day."

He laughed. "Not that restaurant."

They walked down the muggy street and headed toward the sounds and bright lights of Valhalla's Throne. The tall brick building came into view. Edison light bulbs flashed on the marquee atop the building. Lively music poured out the front door, and patrons lined up outside waiting for a seat.

Thor walked to the front of the line, and the bouncer let them through.

"Thor, want some company in there?"

Thor turned to find a Helmarked named Deena ogling him.

"Thanks," he said. "I'm set."

She looked Elle up and down. "I'm always up for a threesome."

Thor's hand tightened on Elle's at the thought of someone else touching her- even a woman.

He ushered Elle into the club. "We're good."

"WHAT'S A THREESOME?" ELLE ASKED AS THEY STEPPED INSIDE.

Thor coughed. "Uh..."

But Elle stopped listening almost as soon as he spoke. The scent of smoke and wood filled Elle's nostrils, bringing back memories of Muspelheim, and for a moment, she froze. The scents and sounds reminded her of her father's great hall.

All around her, men and other beings played games like darts or cards. Women in small, poofy skirts and little more than a bra delivered drinks and food. They wore copious amounts of makeup and bright lipstick, and each one had feathers in her hair that matched her outfit. The women smiled and laughed with the men, touching them, rubbing their shoulders, ruffling their hair. The women were of every shape, size, and color. Several of the women sported heavy leathery wings folded on their backs. A couple more had long pointy tails poking out underneath their skirts. More than half of the women had horns in various sizes and colors. But strangely enough, the most interesting women in the place were the ones who appeared completely mortal. Like the patrons of the Raven Weaver. The ones she would never have been able to tell were anything more than human.

"Are you alright?" Thor asked.

Elle swallowed hard and nodded. The whole thing screamed of a male aesthetic. Deep leather chairs. Dark smoky wood. Rustic red brick walls. Metal ceilings with beams exposed. Dim lighting made everything more mysterious and sensual.

"Thor!"

Elle turned, and a mountainous man lumbered over and pulled Thor into a bear hug.

Thor patted the man on the back. "Come on, Baldur. It's only been a couple weeks since we've seen each other. It's not a lifetime."

"I can't help it. It's just nice to see you, brother." Baldur set Thor back on his feet and turned to Elle. "And who is this?"

Thor took her hand. "Elle, this is Baldur, my brother."

"A pleasure to meet you, Elle." Baldur held out his tree-stump-sized arms for a hug, but Thor set his hand on Baldur's chest.

"No."

Baldur's light eyes sparkled as a smile twisted up the corners of his mouth. "Are you serious?"

Thor's eyes flashed, and Baldur backed up a step.

Wow. He hadn't been kidding when he'd said he would fight his brothers for her.

"All right. All right. No need to get all powered up." Baldur chuckled and held out his hand to her. "Nice to meet you, Elle."

Elle shook his massive calloused hand. "And you, Baldur."

Baldur was a bushy mountain man. Dark hair shaved on the sides and braided on top and down his back. Tattoos covered most of his exposed skin, and he sported a scruffy beard, which made him feel like a giant bear. Even so, she had to admit he was extremely handsome.

"Everyone is already in the house. Even Loki brought a female. A feisty one. I like her. I think he might have finally met his match."

Elle smiled, knowing exactly how feisty Val was. But then her smile fell… were Val and Loki… together? But Val hated Loki. Or did she? They hadn't talked much since the meeting at Frigg's, and when they had, it had only been about Thor. So, was it possible that Val and Loki...

Thor led Elle through the bar to a red velvet curtain, beyond which lay another room. Inside the second room, a stage stood at the end, and half a dozen girls dressed in frilly skirts, corsets, and tall black hats danced, sang, and shook their bodies at the men cheering from their plush seats. Thor pulled her through the theater to another room. The new room again featured a stage with dancing girls, but they wore only skirts and hats. Elle turned from them as Thor led her to yet another room.

"How many rooms does this place have?"

"Dozens," Thor answered.

In the next room, the girls wore only hats.

Thor pulled her in tight to his side. "Sorry, this is the only way to Dad's personal rooms."

Elle nodded and kept her eyes on the floor as they reached a door and Thor knocked. After a moment, the door opened, and an imposing man stood in the doorway.

He glared at them. "Thor."

"Fenrir."

The tall man with eyes the color of glowing coals stepped aside and let them in. Elle had never met Fenrir, but she recognized him from the legends. Son of Loki, Fenrir was a werewolf more feral than humane. And he looked exactly like he'd been portrayed.

The room they walked into threw Elle for a moment. She'd expected another room decorated like the club on the other side of the front door, but it in no way resembled Valhalla's Throne.

The space opened up like a private house tucked behind the world. Exposed timber beams ran the length of the ceiling, their light grain polished to a muted honey sheen. The cream-colored walls held various abstract paintings. The floors were a creamy stone, and a thick white rug anchored the center of the room with a huge glass coffee table filled with water where two beautiful koi fish swam back and forth. The air tasted different as well, no cigarette haze, no spilled mead. Just the mineral coolness of stone walls, fresh water, and the rich, fatty scent of roasting meat that made her stomach growl.

As Fenrir closed the door, even the music of the club shut out as if it didn't exist. An ample leather sectional hosted half a dozen people. Large soft-looking pillows in golds and silvers adorned every few feet of the couch, along with a shimmery plush blanket.

Val and Loki sat at a sleek metal bar on the left side of the room, and Frigg stood behind serving drinks.

Behind the sectional, a wall of French doors stood open, leading into what appeared to be a yard of some kind. Odin tended to a deep fire pit, cooking meat and drinking from a mug while talking to two men. It was strange because they weren't outside, yet looking at where Odin cooked, she would have sworn it was a backyard on Midgard. Lush grass, flowering shrubs, and even several blossoming trees rustled in a slight breeze. Two ravens circled above Odin's head, swooping at the meat every once in a while. And two large wolves lounged on the grass, tails swishing as they watched the invaders of their territory.

Every inch of the space was different from what she'd expected from the Norse god Odin.

"Elle." Frigg moved toward them with a broad smile on her face. Her light pink tunic dress swished around her as she moved toward them. She hugged Elle and then Thor. "I'm glad you two came."

"Thank you for having me," Elle said.

Frigg smiled at her and squeezed her arm. "Would you like a drink?"

"Sparkling water, please," said Elle.

"Ale," said Thor.

Frigg nodded and headed back to the bar.

"Is this where your dad lives?" asked Elle.

"Most of us live where we work. Makes it easier." Thor studied her for a minute and then chuckled. “Not what you expected?”

She shook her head. “Not at all.”

“Yeah, we were all surprised by the change.”

One of the men out with Odin walked inside.

"Thor!" He jogged over and hugged Thor.

"Hey Meili, this is Elle. Elle, this is my brother Meili."

Meili shook Elle's hand with a firm grip. "It's nice to meet you, Elle. I don't think I've met any of Thor's friends since-"

Thor coughed. "Yes, well, until Elle, I haven't had anyone I wanted to meet you lot."

Meili snorted.

"I smell metal and melancholy; it must mean Thor has arrived." The second man entered behind Meili.

Thor smiled, and the two hugged. The man's eyes were the palest shade of blue, almost white.

"Elle, this is my brother Hödr."

Hödr ran his fingers over her hand, then bent down and sniffed it. Elle looked at Thor, but Thor just smiled.

Hödr kissed the back of her hand and stopped. He stayed still for a tense moment before straightening. "Even a blind man can see her beauty," said Hödr, letting go of her.

"Th... Thank you," she stammered. Elle swallowed hard.

Though his eyes didn't work, she sensed he saw straight through to her soul. The sensation sent a chill down her neck.

"Chow's ready," Odin called.

The group headed out to what Elle had taken for a patio, only to find it was a giant room with a tall ceiling, where white fabric and perfectly round, glowing lights strung across beams created a beautiful, romantic effect. At the far end of the room stood an enormous rustic wooden table that looked like an ancient tree.

Thor walked her over and pulled out a seat for her. Val slid into a chair next to her, her gaze intense. Thor chuckled and sat on Elle's other side.

For the first time, Val appeared... happy? No. Not happy. Content maybe. And to Elle's surprise, Loki's hand slid onto Val's thigh as he seated himself next to her. Val brushed Loki's hand away. He chuckled before putting his hand right back and winking at Elle. Val didn't push his hand away again.

Well, that answered that question. There was definitely something between Val and Loki.

CHAPTER TWELVE

The dinner with his family went better than Thor expected. Fenrir didn't try to rip Vidarr apart for the first time. Neither Hödr nor Baldur brought up the fact that it was Loki's fault that Hödr had shot Baldur. Frigg and Odin talked like old friends, not exes. And Hermódr didn't try to reveal any of the family's ancient secret messages. Even his brother Váli didn't try spouting his peace, yoga, and tea philosophy to everyone. All in all, it was peaceful.

When dessert was served, Thor leaned over to Elle. "Are you enjoying yourself?"

She smiled at him. "I never knew family gatherings could be like this."

"Noisy?"

"Fun. You and your family are... normal. No shouting. No fights. No force watching couples have sex."

"What?" *Who would do such a thing?*

"Oh, I was never a participant, not that anyone would have wanted me. But I was forced to remain in the room."

Thor gripped the arm of his chair tight enough that he thought it might crack. "I said you didn't need to tell me about your past, but if you do, I can't promise you I won't kill every person who ever hurt you."

She gave him a tight smile.

They finished their dessert, and Elle and Meili began clearing the dishes.

"Let me help." Thor stood, but she took the plate from his hand.

"You sit. I can do this."

"But you're my guest."

"Then, as your guest, I expect you to give me what I want. And what I want is for you to sit while I clear the dishes." She turned on her heels and headed for the kitchen.

Thor watched her go and sipped his ale. He loved the soft way her hips swished as she moved. So graceful. So mesmerizing. And in a red silk dress, it was like watching flames.

Watching her and Meili standing at the kitchen sink, washing dishes and talking, she fit in naturally. As if she'd always been there, not meeting most of them for the first time. Better than he'd ever fit in, and he'd had a lot of time to try.

His family moved about the space. Several of his brothers began a game of cards while a few others went to sit around the fire pit outside.

Thor took a swig of ale, watching Elle across the room and wondering how it had taken him so long to find her. A second mug appeared in front of him, and the chair next to him pulled out, as Hödr sat down.

Hödr stared at Thor with his sightless eyes. It still surprised

Thor how well his brother had adjusted to losing his sight. He'd worried about Hödr when they'd first moved to Helheim, but he'd become accustomed to it quickly, even taking to opening his own small library of ancient texts from different civilizations, and teaching at a local college in Los Angeles twice a week.

"I'm surprised you came." Hödr swigged his ale.

"It was time." Thor's gaze traveled back to Elle, who smiled and laughed at something Meili said. Jealousy coursed through him, wanting to be the one who made Elle laugh. The only one.

"You care for this one," Hödr said finally. "You care a lot."

Thor glanced at his brother. It still astounded him how someone who had no physical sight saw so much. They'd never spoken about it, but he often wondered if Frigg had bespelled him because she felt guilty that Váli had been born only to kill him and avenge the death of Baldur.

"I do," Thor admitted.

Hödr nodded and laid his hand on Thor's shoulder. "It's good you've found happiness and made peace with the past. You would have missed out on something amazing with her if you hadn't."

Thor blinked at Hödr. "What do you mean?"

"With Surtr. Forgiving him for Ragnarök, and realizing it had to come about. I mean, if nothing else, it allowed us to come here, and you to find her."

Thor's mind whirled. "What are you talking about? I haven't forgiven Surtr. I will still avenge us for what he did."

Hödr's eyes narrowed. "Is she aware of that?"

Thor looked at Hödr, then at Elle, and back to Hödr. Dread snaked through his gut.

"Why would Elle care about my plans to avenge us with Surtr?"

Hödr's eyes widened, and an expression of guilt mixed with shame crossed his face.

Thor's throat dried.

Elle's abnormally warm skin. Her raw, untapped power. A strange connection between them. Her flaming hair. The golden flecks in her eyes. The way Frigg had taken her in. The way Odin had known her. The way Val didn't seem to like him, and her need to protect Elle from him. And now Hödr. Hödr, who couldn't see with eyes, but saw beyond what others did.

Frigg's words floated back to him.

"Be careful."

"I am not going to hurt her."

"I didn't mean her. I meant you."

No. It wasn't possible. Couldn't be.

"She's a fire giant," Thor said.

Hödr stared at him unblinkingly, pain crossing his face.

"Tell me," Thor commanded.

Hödr didn't speak.

Thor grabbed his wrist and squeezed. "Tell me what you saw." It wasn't a command, but it came close.

Hödr sighed and removed his wrist from Thor's grip before running it through his hair. "She's Surtr's daughter. Can't you sense the power flowing through her? The faint smell of smokiness to her skin."

Thor got up from the table so fast his chair tipped backward and crashed to the floor. His heartbeat slammed inside him. His temples throbbed as the lights flickered.

Everyone stopped moving. Lightning crackled outside, and thunder rolled across the top of the building. Time slowed as Elle turned and their eyes connected.

Surtr's daughter. Elle is Surtr's daughter.

The smile she wore fell. Lightning hit the floor next to him, knocking Hödr out of his chair.

"Thor!" Odin yelled. "Enough."

Val jumped in front of Elle. Twin silver and golden blades protruded from her wrist bracelets. Val... *Valkyrie*. How had he not seen it? How had he been blinded?

Loki stepped next to Val, his eyes darkening, and a faint glow of blue magic appeared in his hand.

"Did all of you know?" Thor yelled. "Am I the only one not in on the joke?"

Elle took a step forward, but Meili pulled her back and whispered something in her ear.

Thunder rolled louder above the building.

"Thor." Frigg moved gracefully toward him. "It's not like that. Elle's mother was a dear friend who Surtr kidnapped at Ragnarök. We thought she had died. When Val sent me word about Elle, I had to help. I loved her mother like a sister. And Val is a Valkyrie. One of our own."

Thor looked to her. "You. You're the one who told me to come to your masquerade. You knew she would be there. You knew we would meet."

"Your fate and the fate of the fire giants have been tied together since the beginning of time. Did I know it would be Surtr's daughter who would heal your heart? No. I only knew someone would. And that someone would be from the house of Surtr."

"And you," he said to Odin. "You knew who she was when you saw us together, didn't you?"

Odin crossed his sinewy arms over his chest. "Yes."

Thor's heart pounded so loud it rivaled the thunder booming overhead. They knew. They all knew. And no one told him.

His gaze met Elle's, and tears welled in her eyes. He wanted to go to her. To tell her it didn't matter. He didn't care who her father was. That he loved her and that was all that mattered. But he couldn't.

Thor grabbed his hammer from inside his jacket and pointed it skyward before anyone spoke. His feet lifted from the floor and disappeared into the sky.

Elle stood paralyzed. Unable to do anything more than watch Thor disappear. She wasn't sure how he'd found out the truth; she was only upset that he hadn't found out about it from her. She should have told him the truth. Should have forced him to listen and let her tell him who she was. Maybe he would have reacted the same, maybe he wouldn't have. It didn't matter; all that mattered was that he thought his entire family had lied to him. That *she* had lied to him. And now… he was gone.

Elle set down the dish towel she'd been using and walked toward the exit.

Val grasped her arm. Elle stared at her for a moment.

"I should have told him."

Val's mouth opened and closed several times. Her eyes held compassion Elle had never seen before.

Elle peered around the group and offered a weak smile. "Thank you all for a lovely meal. I think I should go." She curtsied low, though every fiber of her body told her she wasn't worthy of anything more than groveling for their forgiveness.

"Elle, stay," said Frigg. "Thor will move beyond this. Trust me."

Elle nodded. "Thank you, Lady Frigg, but I think I'd like to go back to my apartment."

"I'll take you," said Val.

Elle held up her hand, stopping her friend. "I don't want you to miss out."

"Let me take you," Meili offered.

Elle shook her head. "I'll be fine."

She turned for the door, her limbs heavy and her gut hollow. She'd lost him. She'd been so afraid she'd lose him if she told him, but not telling him had been a thousand times worse. Now she had ruined not only her relationship with Thor but also his family's relationships as well.

Frigg walked to her side and linked her arm with Elle's. "I'll go. I have to go pick up a few things at the Raven Weaver anyway."

Elle wanted to protest, but Frigg was right; she shouldn't go alone, plus she wasn't sure she'd find her way back.

"Thank you, Lady Frigg."

"Frigg. Or Auntie Frigg, if you prefer. I meant what I said. Your mother was like a sister to me."

Elle nodded.

The two walked out the door and back through Valhalla's Throne to Helheim. Elle didn't notice anyone or anything on her way. All she saw was the look in Thor's eyes when he realized who she was. Nothing had ever cut her so deep. Not even a beating from her father had hurt as much as the pain and rage in Thor's eyes.

"Would you like me to take you to Thor's so you can talk?"

"No," Elle said. "Thank you, but I think it's best that I give him some space."

"He'll come around," said Frigg as they walked onto the street. "He's in shock. But he will realize what he feels for you is real, and he'll calm down. If he can forgive Loki for everything he's ever done, Thor can forgive you for not telling him who your father is."

Elle's gut clenched, and tears welled again. She wasn’t so sure.

They walked down the dark street, and with every step, a sense of dread washed over her. She didn't know what to think. What to feel. What to do.

"Thor's always had a lot put on his shoulders, and the destruction of Asgard is something he's never been able to forgive himself for."

"But it was prophesied. Nothing could have changed it."

"True. But you must also realize Thor isn't used to losing. He was the golden son. Odin's favorite. That meant in his eyes to keep favor, he had to be the best, always."

"No one can do that."

Frigg nodded. "That's the pressure Odin placed on him every single day. To be the best. To be the hero of Asgard. The savior of his people. And in Thor's eyes, he failed."

"No wonder he's cut himself off so much."

Frigg sighed. "I've tried for centuries to get him to realize he is more than Thor Odinson. I had hoped coming here and getting out of Valhalla would help him find his own path. Be who he wanted to be. And in a small way, it has, though not completely. But when you arrived... For the first time, I saw the possibility of a future for him. You are exactly what he needs, Elle. He will see that."

Elle gave Frigg a stiff smile as they reached the entrance to The Raven Weaver. She hoped more than anything Frigg was right, but she couldn't bank on it. In the whole of her life, she'd never gotten anything she dreamed of.

Elle walked through the portal to Midgard. She hiked up the stairs, her body heavier than ever. She paused, noticing Heimdall wasn't in his usual spot, but didn't think much of it. Even Heimdall needed a break every once in a while.

She continued heading to her apartment. Halfway up the stairs, she took off her heels, giving her feet a much-needed break from the torture.

She stared at the floor as she headed toward her door and paused, remembering what lay inside. Her unmade bed. Memories of making love to Thor. The scent of him on her pillows. The emptiness where his arms held her close. All things that would pummel her until there was nothing left.

She thought about going to Val's room instead, but decided against it. She didn't want to be a burden if Val brought Loki home with her.

Elle pushed open her door, and the scent that hit had her backing up in a heartbeat, but she wasn't fast enough. Before she could scream, strong arms covered her mouth and yanked her into the apartment.

CHAPTER THIRTEEN

Thor sat on the shattered edge of what remained of the Bifröst and stared out at the remaining floating shards of Asgard.

The bridge beneath him lay a ruin of fractured prismatic crystal, each broken slab still humming with residual energy that vibrated up through his thighs. Where the Bifröst had once stretched in an unbroken arc of rainbow-hued brilliance, now only jagged stumps jutted into the void, their edges dulled to a milky iridescence like old bruises on glass.

Beyond them, the remnants of Asgard drifted in silence- towers snapped at their midsections, golden domes caved inward, whole sections of palace wall tumbling in slow, weightless rotation through a sky that wasn't sky. Just an endless expanse of deep indigo streaked with veins of silver dust where stars used to anchor themselves.

Thor pressed his palms flat against the crystalline surface, feeling the cold bite through his calloused fingers- hands roughened by centuries of gripping Mjölnir's handle and, more recently, by wrenches and engine grease. His boots dangled over the edge where the bridge ended, into nothingness. A colorless void of metal and stone, but tasted like death and grief.

The absolute silence pressed against his eardrums and made the blood in his own veins sound deafening. The only motion came from the continued drifting fragments of his former home: a carved lintel spinning a hundred yards out, still bearing the rune for *protection* in flaking gold leaf. A chunk of courtyard flagstone, trailing soil, and the withered roots of what had once been his mother's garden.

The cold wasn't like Midgard cold, wasn't weather. It was the absence of temperature, as if the place had lost its reason to generate heat. It settled into his shoulders, crept beneath the jacket collar against the column of his neck. It burrowed in his knees, and in the old ache along his left side where Surt's blade had found a gap in his armor during Ragnarök itself.

Thor's hands curled against the Bifröst's broken edge until the crystal bit into his skin.

It'd been a century since he'd been there. At first, he'd not been able to bring himself to see it after it'd happened. But while in Valhalla, he'd found himself there often. Staring off, trying to figure out what he'd done wrong. How he could have fixed what happened. After centuries, he'd finally stopped. But strangely, when he'd left the family dinner, the Bifröst was where Mjölnir had taken him.

He blew out a deep sigh. Surtr's daughter. Elle was Surtr's daughter. Were they all planning on keeping it from him? If it hadn't been for Hödr...

Thor threw his hands over his face and lay back on the Bifröst. A fire giant. His mortal enemy. The one being he was unable to beat. And the one woman who'd opened his heart after being closed for so long, ends up being the daughter of his enemy.

"I thought you'd be here," said a voice.

Thor looked up into a pair of bright golden eyes. "Of course you did. You see everything."

Heimdall chuckled and sat next to Thor. "True. At least I still do when it comes to you."

Thor stared out at a crumbling piece of mural for a moment before it collided with another piece and exploded into dust. "Did you see her? Elle?"

Heimdall shrugged.

"And did you see that she was my 'one'?"

Heimdall stared at him for a moment. "Is she your 'one'?"

Thor blew out a harsh breath. The answer jumped into his mind without a second of hesitation. His chest squeezed. In all the fates, why? Why her? Why was she the one?

"I will take that as a yes," Heimdall said.

Thor groaned.

"This news makes you unhappy? Interesting. I didn't think it possible for you to be more miserable than you already were. To be honest, most men find it a happy occasion to find the one they were meant to be with. Especially immortals who have waited thousands of years."

"It was, until I found out she was Surtr's daughter."

Heimdall shrugged. "So what? She isn't Surtr."

"But-"

"But what? Does it change who she is? Why you fell for her? How you feel about her?"

"I... don't know," Thor admitted.

Heimdall stayed silent for a long while, both of them staring off at the swirling void before them where their home world used to be.

"I can tell you this, Odinson," Heimdall finally said. "For as much as you have suffered over Ragnarök, that girl has suffered a thousand times over at the hands of her father."

Thor remembered the few things she'd told him. And then remembered the way she'd frozen when the human had grabbed her. How she'd flinched at every turn, afraid of being hit. The thought made Thor's gut clench and sent a spike of rage coursing through him. Lightning cracked across the sky.

"Have you stopped to think why she ran from her home?"

"She told me of some of her abuse."

"And I can attest to as much as she told you, there are a thousand things she didn't. When the girl started a month ago, she was more scared than a rabbit in a snare. She jumped at the slightest sound. There wasn't one time that the door didn't open that she didn't duck behind the bar and hide. If someone moved too fast, she cowered. She's been getting better day by day, yet I've still seen her fear. But these last few days with you, she changed. She isn't as scared anymore. She holds herself differently, and her smile meets her eyes. You did that for her, as she's done for you. Are you going to let that go because of this?" He gestured around. "When are you going to stop letting something you couldn't control then and can't change now ruin your life?"

"It's my fault-"

"No. It's not, Thor. Why can't you understand? Why do you torture yourself? No one else does. No one blames you. And if you are being honest with yourself, aren't you at least a small amount relieved? Ragnarök set you free. It set us all free. Stop being a gigantic baby and move on."

Thor snorted. "You think I'm being a baby?"

"About this, yes. Odin loves you most. He expects the most from you, but even he knew Ragnarök was inevitable. And if you think about it. Really, truly, look deep, past the pain, past the guilt, isn't there a part of you that is glad it happened? Glad you got to move on. Glad you no longer have to be Thor, the savior of Asgard and humanity alike. You can just be Thor, motorcycle mechanic, and lover of Elle."

Thor hated it, but when he searched deep, Heimdall was right. If it hadn't been for Ragnarök, he would still be fighting. Working to earn the love of people he didn't know. Constantly at his father's beck and call. Never who he wanted to be.

"I'll leave you with your thoughts," said Heimdall. "But if you want one last piece of advice, I'll give it to you."

"Does it matter whether I want it or not?"

Heimdall snorted. "No."

"Thought not."

"Thor, this is your one true shot at finding the person who makes you happy. Someone meant for you. To make you whole. To give you the life you both deserve. Together. Are you willing to give that up for both of you? You aren't the only one hurting. A relationship goes two ways. Meaning, you are her fated mate as much as she is yours. What will it do to her if you don't get over it?"

Thor tossed a sliver of the Bifröst into the void. "Even Tanngrisnir and Tanngnjóstr love her."

Heimdall chuckled. "Well, if you don't want to listen to me, listen to them. Those goats haven't been wrong about anyone."

"They only tolerate me," he said.

Heimdall stood. "Like I said, never wrong."

Thor laughed.

Heimdall smiled and walked several feet along the Bifröst before disappearing.

Thor stared out at the blackness. Maybe it was time he forgot about Surtr, Ragnarök, and everything else and moved forward. It'd been over a thousand years. Didn't he deserve happiness? Better yet, didn't Elle?

CHAPTER FOURTEEN

Thor dropped into the upper hallway of the Raven Weaver, a few doors down from Elle's apartment. He stared down the hall for several minutes, trying to formulate what he would say. Apologies were a given. And let her tell him her story. He was still conflicted over who she was, and he wasn't sure he'd be able to forgive her, or his family, so quickly for deceiving him, but one thing was for sure- he couldn't lose Elle.

Thor took a deep breath and walked to Elle's door. He lifted his hand to knock, but it stood ajar. The hairs raised on his arm. He knocked, and the door creaked open a few inches. No sound floated out of the darkness. He knocked again, and the door opened wider.

"Elle?" Thor waited. "Elle, it's Thor."

No reply.

He wondered for a moment if she'd gone down to the bar.

Thor stepped into the apartment. "Elle?"

He walked to the lamp and turned it on. His stomach dropped

like he'd eaten a boulder. The table and chairs had been flipped. The couch pillows scattered across the floor, and Elle's high heels lay on either side of the kitchen area.

"Elle!" Thor tore through the apartment to the bedroom. The bed remained as disheveled as when he'd left.

"Elle!" He ran into the bathroom.

Nothing.

Thor rushed back to the hallway and down the stairs to the Raven Weaver. He stopped at the bottom and scanned the bar. He caught Heimdall speaking to Val and Loki and headed for them.

"Have you seen Elle?" he demanded.

Val jumped to her feet. "She's upstairs."

Thor shook his head. "Her apartment looks like there's been a fight."

Val fled quicker than Thor thought possible. Loki followed after.

"Can you see her?" he asked Heimdall.

Heimdall's eyes glazed over and turned white. They moved rapidly back and forth and then cleared. "She is on Muspelheim."

Shit.

Thor grabbed Mjölnir, but Heimdall laid his hand on Thor's arm. "Not here."

Thor glanced around at the mortals and headed for the portal.

He made it through, and Frigg spotted him.

"What's wrong?" she asked, moving to his side.

"Elle's been taken to Muspelheim."

A frightened expression planted itself on Frigg's face. "We need your father."

"I need to go. Who knows what is happening to her." He raised Mjölnir.

"Thor, wait." Frigg grabbed him. "You can't just show up there. You need your father."

"No," said Thor. "I need Elle." He threw his arm in the air and shot upward.

ELLE STARED OUT THE WINDOW INTO THE ASHEN FIELDS OF Muspelheim. In the distance, a volcano erupted, spewing ash and lava over the ground, much like Surtr had done the moment she'd set foot back in the castle.

It'd been Thadren's men who'd tracked her down and Thadren himself who had brought her back. Rather than be angry with her over her disappearance, he seemed amused. Surtr, however, had been anything but.

She'd only been spared a thrashing or death sentence because Thadren had promised to still take her as his bride. To which Surtr had immediately sent Elle to her room to be prepared for the wedding.

Elle stared off as the servants stripped her down and scrubbed her with coarse brushes. She didn't give them the satisfaction of seeing her shiver from the cool water they used. She stood, head held high, staring out the window.

She had considered fighting them. Considered breaking out of the castle and making a run for it, but where would she go? And more than that, what was the point? Thor hated her, and if she couldn't have Thor, it didn't matter what happened to her. At least with Thadren, she knew what to expect. And he'd not been violent to her like her father. But if he was... well, she wasn't going to take the abuse anymore. She may not be able to control her magic all the way, but she could control it enough to do some damage.

The servants pulled on white undergarments and a gown and tried to move Elle to a chair, but Elle resisted.

"If you want me to do something, you ask me," she snapped. "Politely. You don't shove me about like a farm animal."

The women looked at her, then at each other. One of them inclined her head.

"If you would sit, Princess Sutrelle, we will brush out your hair and braid it for you."

"You may brush it," said Sutrelle. "But I don't want it braided."

Again, the women nodded.

Sutrelle walked to the chair and sat, letting her long hair flow down her back. The show of assertion had Elle ready to bite the skin off her fingers; instead, she looked down at her gown. The iridescent dragonsilk fabric was some of the hardest in the nine realms to procure, and she was sure it hadn't been obtained by her father.

"Where did this dress come from?"

"Prince Thadren brought it for you."

"As a welcome home gift for your wedding."

Elle bit the inside of her cheek. She wondered if her father was aware he was marrying her off to someone so generous. He could have married her off to any number of monsters like himself, but surprisingly, he hadn't. Which meant one thing- Thadren was considerably more powerful than her father liked to admit.

"We've finished, Princess. Are you sure you wouldn't like us to braid it?"

Elle stood from the chair and walked back to the window. "No, thank you."

"Then we will take our leave if you don't need anything else."

The volcano continued to spew forth its destruction. If she got lucky, it would flow down to the border and destroy Muspelheim castle.

The door opened, and the two women's footsteps left as a heavy set of footsteps entered. She didn't need to look to know one of her father's guards had come in to make sure she didn't try anything. The most she could do now was take what she'd learned from Thor and Val and try to make the best of what was about to happen to her.

IN THE GREAT HALL, ALL THE HEAVY STONE TABLES HAD BEEN ANGLED sideways, and an aisle had been made through the center of them to the head table, where her father sat with Thadren. The hall reeked of sulfur and roasted meat, the air so thick with heat it pressed against her bare arms like a second skin. Torches of volcanic glass lined the walls, their flames shades of amber and deep crimson, throwing distorted shadows across the vaulted ceiling. The stone floor radiated warmth through the thin soles of her slippers, each step a reminder that Muspelheim's fire burned beneath everything, always. Rows of fire giants filled the tables on either side of the aisle- massive figures with skin like cracked basalt, their expressions a mixture of disdain and greed. At the head table, Sutr occupied his throne like a mountain refusing to erode. Surtr stood ten feet of menace, his skin split with veins of molten orange that pulsed at his jaw and knuckles. His beard smoldered, each ember-tipped hair curling against the black of his breastplate. Those burning eyes, twin furnaces set deep in a face carved from cruelty, fixed on her the moment she crossed the threshold. The only difference in the hall, besides the layout, was the addition of a familiar, smaller silver throne that sat next to Thadren's.

Mother's throne.

She'd never been allowed to sit in it before. In fact, her father had hidden it away when she was young after seeing her playing on it once. She swallowed at the sight of it and wondered if things would have turned out differently for her if her mother had survived.

Thadren sat with his hands resting flat on the table, his posture a calculated display of ease. But the moment he spotted her, he smiled, broad and toothy. Not leeringly, but more genuine happiness at seeing her. Maybe life with him wouldn't be as painful as she thought it might. If he actually held affection for her, she could use that to her advantage.

His muscular frame was packed into ceremonial armor of hammered bronze and dark iron, which creaked when he shifted. His oiled, rust-colored beard had been braided for the occasion, threaded with thin chains. The cracks along his jaw and throat glowed a dull orange, brighter than usual, though his expression remained pleasant.

Elle stood in the doorway awaiting instruction. The familiar smell of men, sweat, meat, and fire made her stomach sour as a trickle of anxiety threaded through her stomach. She wanted to get this over with. The one good thing about leaving with Thadren would be that she wouldn't be subjected to the foul odor of her father's house anymore.

After a minute, Thadren stood, and her father's guard prodded Elle in the back with his sword. Elle rounded on him.

"Do not touch me," she said with enough venom to make Val proud.

The guard's eyes narrowed, but she continued to stare straight at him, daring him to do something. Her magic bubbled and churned inside her, swirling close to the surface, ready for her command, but the man looked away, and Elle turned back to the gathered crowd.

She needed to keep her wits about her. She couldn't lose it now. If she lost control and her father saw what she could do… who knew what would happen.

What a wedding day. The same men who'd always looked down on her. The same tables, food, and hall. No flower or piece of white cloth adorned the place to show that the day was more special than any other. In the dress Thadren had procured for her, she felt considerably overdressed for her own wedding.

Surtr finally pushed to his feet, and everyone else followed suit. She assumed that was her cue to move. She took a deep breath and strode forward, head up, eyes straight on her father. He studied her with a mixture of anger and surprise.

Good. Let him be surprised. Let him see I won't allow him to treat me the same way anymore.

The one thing being with Thor had done for her was to show her her worth and what she deserved. If she never got anything else from him, she was grateful to him for that. She only wished she'd been able to do something for him in return.

Elle reached the head table, and Thadren walked around it to stand next to her. For the first time, she noted how old her father looked. Deep wrinkles and dozens of scars etched into his face. His bare arms still bore great, bulky muscles, but the deep, ashen skin had begun to lose its elasticity, sagging in places. Even his eyes appeared more sunken in and hooded by puffy eyelids. Only the bright flames of his eyes and beard showed any semblance of youth.

For the first time, she realized why her father was marrying her off to Thadren. Not because Thadren needed her father's armies, but because her father needed Thadren's strength. With no sons of his own, Surtr wanted someone as strong as himself, if not stronger, to replace him someday on the throne of Muspelheim. Someone of his choosing.

In an instant, all the fear Elle held for her father vanished. The realization that she held the power had never occurred to her. As much as Surtr would hate to admit it, he needed Elle. Needed her to be able to broker the deal with Thadren, to prolong his legacy.

Something clicked.

"Great warriors of Muspelheim. We are here tonight to bear witness to the union of Princess Sutrelle, daughter of Surtr, to Prince Thadren, son of Throndel. With this union, the two halves of our kingdom will be united and heal the rift that has split our people for the last thousand years. And when our people are once again all one, united under the banner of House Surtr, with Prince Thadren heir to the throne of all Muspelheim, we will once again set out to conquer what is left of the nine realms."

Cheering and banging arose around the room at Surtr's words. Many of the attendees raised their flagons of ale and gulped them down.

Surtr held up his hand. "It is my honor to welcome Prince Thadren to our castle and to offer him my daughter, Princess Sutrelle, to be his wife, body, mind, and soul."

Thadren bowed to Surtr. "And it is my great honor to take

Princess Sutrelle, daughter of Surtr, to be my wife, body, mind, and soul."

Surtr's gaze turned on Sutrelle, hard and expressionless. "Princess Sutrelle, I offer you to Prince Thadren, to be his wife in body, mind, and soul."

It struck Elle how one-sided the marriage vows were. She was being offered up as the sacrificial lamb to Thadren, but he wasn't offering anything to her. The vows alone explained so much.

A moment passed and then another. Surtr's eyes narrowed, and the flames in his beard grew longer and brighter.

"Princess Sutrelle, I offer you to Prince Thadren, to be his wife in body, mind, and soul," he repeated.

Elle lifted her chin. "No."

Surtr's eyes flashed. "There is no 'no' allowed, Sutrelle."

"No," she said louder.

A buzz of whispers raced around the crowd.

"You have no say. Sutrelle, daughter of Surtr-"

"No! If you want Thadren to be your heir, adopt him, marry him, I don't care, but I will not be a pawn in your plans any longer."

Surtr raised his hand to strike her, but Elle raised hers as well, allowing her magic to flow over her hands and arms for the first time in front of anyone but Val.

"Go ahead," she dared him. "Try to strike me, and I will show you what I've inherited from both my mother and you."

Surtr froze. "Your mother's magic."

Elle didn't respond.

"But you can't use it. You've never been taught."

"Do you want to find out?" she challenged.

His flames flared. "Are you threatening me, girl?"

The magic within Elle surged, swelling with every heartbeat like a vibrant storm gathering strength inside her. It unfurled like the petals of a blossom, spreading its warmth and light to every corner of her until her hand shimmered with a soft radiance. The air around her buzzed, and her skin tingled.

"No. I am warning you," she said. "I will no longer take the abuse you have meted out on me my entire life. I will not be my mother and die under the weight of your hatred. I may be the daughter of Surtr, but I am also the daughter of Aelena, Priestess of Asgard."

"How dare you-"

"How dare I? How dare you?" Her magic spiked as her temper flared. *Interesting.* "How dare you try to sell me off like a prize goat? I won't be bullied by you anymore. I will marry whom I choose and when I choose, and you have no say in it."

"I'll kill you, you little bitch," Surtr roared.

Thunder suddenly rolled over the castle so loud the windows rattled, and several pieces of décor crashed to the ground.

Surtr's hand dropped, and Thadren, as well as most of the audience, turned as the giant stone doors to the great hall burst inward, the stone exploding across the floor, dust flying inward like a swarm of bugs.

In ran two enormous goats pulling a golden chariot the size of a small dragon. The goats ran straight for Elle. Thadren backed up as Tanngrisnir and Tanngnjóstr slammed into the head table, throwing it backward and tipping over the three thrones. Surtr managed to jump out of the way before being bowled over as well.

Tanngrisnir and Tanngnjóstr reached Elle, their sizes that of juvenile elephants. They raised up on their back legs and bleated so loudly that several tables of giants backed away from them. They dropped back down, and both nudged at Elle with their noses.

Shock mixed with joy as she pet their noses and kissed them. The goats formed a barricade in front of Elle like two furry protective mountains between her and her father.

"Get me my sword!" Surtr bellowed. "We'll have goat meat for a week."

"No!" Elle ducked under her protectors and aimed her hands at her father, ready to attack.

"I wouldn't if I were you." Thor stepped out of the chariot in full Asgardian armor, pointing Mjölnir at him. Mjölnir had morphed into its true form, so massive that Thor's hands barely closed around the hilt.

"Thor Odinson, finally, you've come, so I can finish what I started."

He was there. He'd come for her. Or… had he? Maybe he hadn't come to rescue her. Maybe he'd come to kill her father and leave her to rot with Thadren.

Thor's lightning gaze turned from Surtr to Elle. Thunder cracked across the sky, and lightning struck the floor on either side of him.

Elle swallowed hard as his lightning-streaked eyes sought her out. His face remained unreadable as he stalked toward her like a fierce predator.

He stopped at her side, and it took everything inside Elle to keep from throwing her arms around him.

Tanngrisnir stamped his feet and bumped Thor. Thor growled and shoved him away.

"Stop it," Thor grumbled.

Elle's heart raced, and her magic flared, ready to defend her if necessary.

Thor looked over her, taking in her dress and then looking into her eyes again. Finally, he touched her cheek. "Are you hurt?"

Elle shook her head, unable to form words. Thor was there. He was there… for her. Tears flooded her eyes, and her throat choked closed.

"Unhand Thadren's bride," Surtr bellowed. "I won against you once, Odinson, I can do it again. Only this time I'll make sure you won't come back."

Thadren's bride? Not his daughter. But the property already belongs to Thadren.

"I wouldn't be sure you'll win a second time," said Thor. "This fight has not been prophesied about."

Surtr laughed. "Doesn't make a difference. I did it once. I'll do it again."

Thor threw Mjölnir at Surtr. Surtr grabbed a chair and hurled it at Mjölnir. The chair burst into pieces, and Surtr ducked as Mjölnir bounced off the wall and flew straight back to Thor.

"Unhand her," Surtr yelled again, leaping over the table and yanking the sword from Thadren's side. He pointed the sword at Elle's chest and pushed her out of Thor's grip.

Thor growled but let go of her. Thadren pulled Elle out of the way as Surtr advanced on Thor.

"Come, Odinson. Let me show you once more how easy you are to beat."

Thor laughed. "You only won last time because I was alone. Last time, I didn't have them." He jerked his thumb over his shoulder.

In a flash of light, the entrance to the great hall filled with people. Odin, Frigg, Heimdall, Thor's brothers, and a darkly dressed woman she didn't recognize, as well as Fenrir, stood in full battle armor. Beside them, a portal opened, and Loki and Val stepped through, also armed to fight.

Surtr laughed. "You think you are enough to beat me and my armies? It will be my pleasure to send you, a ragtag group of Asgardians, into oblivion. Even with all your strength, you cannot beat us."

"Your ego hasn't diminished over time," said Odin.

"His undeserved ego," Loki corrected.

"My ego is nothing compared to yours, Loki, son of a *Jötunn*. You should be siding with your own kind. Are you here to stab Asgardians in the back again and help me instead?"

Loki's eyes flashed, and his skin paled to a grayish blue. Two blades appeared in his hands as his clothing turned to native frost giant armor. He took a step forward, but Val stuck out her arm to stop him.

"Not your fight," she said.

"Come on, Asgardians," Surtr taunted. "I will take you all on at once. And then I'll go to what is left of Asgard and obliterate the rest of your rainbow bridge. And there is nothing any of you can do about it."

Odin flung his spear at Surtr, but Surtr caught it and flung it right back. Odin grabbed Frigg around the waist and hoisted her sideways before she was impaled. Thor's brothers swore and pushed forward, shielding their mother.

"Try hurting my mother again, and I'll rip this entire structure down with you still inside," yelled Baldur.

Loki disappeared and reappeared behind Surtr. He drove both blades into Surtr's back, but they melted, and the hilts clattered to the ground at Loki's feet.

"Was that meant to hurt?" Surtr swung around and struck Loki, knocking him across the room.

Val took to the air, her white wings spreading wide, and grabbed Loki before he crashed into the fireplace. Together they tumbled across a table of her father's men, sending them scattering.

Fenrir roared and raced forward. Hermódr went to grab Fenrir but missed, and Fenrir got several yards closer.

"Brother!"

Fenrir stopped moving. "I can take him."

"Sorry, I'm afraid not. But I can," said the woman in black.

The woman wore a skin-tight black dress that shimmered with some type of armor Elle had never seen before. Her ebony hair, slicked back into intricate braids, and she held a shiny, blackened trident, trailing swirling smoke behind her.

A shiver raced through Elle at the sight of the ominous, formidable woman.

For the first time, true fear crossed her father's features.

"You... you can't be here," said Surtr. "You aren't allowed."

The woman shrugged and slithered forward, her movements both provocative and terrifying in their grace. "I spoke to my boss and got special permission to leave my realm. I've never seen him excited about the prospect of someone coming into his realm. He's never met a fire giant before. And you… Well, your reputation precedes you. You've eluded me for too long, Surtr. Your reign is over."

"Go with her," said Thor. "Or we will make you go."

Surtr licked his lips. "Thadren, ready your men."

Thadren looked at Elle, then at Thor's family.

If Thadren decided to fight, Thor and his family might be

injured, and someone could be killed permanently. Someone she cared about.

“Wait," Elle blurted.

All eyes turned to her. She licked her lips and looked straight at Thadren. "As heir to the throne, I will give you Muspelheim, all of it, if you do nothing."

"You have no right to offer that," said Surtr.

"I do. When you leave for Helheim, I will be in charge. And as your successor, I have the right to abdicate the throne and to give it to whomever I deem the strongest and best to lead your people. And I choose Thadren."

Thadren looked as if he were weighing his options. “You do not want the throne?”

“No,” said Elle.

He studied her for a moment and then looked at Thor. “You choose him?”

She nodded.

Thadren’s expression fell for a fraction of a moment, and Elle felt a pang of sadness for him.

“I would have been good to you, Princess,” he said low enough for only her ears. “I would have loved you.”

“I know you would have,” she said. “But, he’s mine. And I am already his.”

Thadren ran a gentle finger down her cheek before pulling his hand away. His expression hardened, and he looked at Surtr. "We will not fight."

Surtr bellowed a guttural roar that reverberated through the cavernous hall. His fiery eyes blazed with unrelenting fury. With a deafening crash, he launched himself at Thadren, the massive blade in his hand gleaming like liquid fire. The ground quaked beneath his weight as he closed the distance in two thunderous strides.

"Thadren! No!" Elle's voice rang out, hands trembling as she summoned her magic. Her chest heaved with exertion, her fingers tingling with raw energy that begged to be unleashed. Her power coursed through her veins, hot and wild. She raised her hands and thrust them forward, releasing a crackling surge of violent energy that illuminated the hall in an otherworldly glow.

But her aim faltered.

The magic seared through the air, missing Surtr by mere inches, and instead collided with her mother's throne behind him.

Surtr froze. His lips curled back into a snarl as he turned to Elle, his eyes locking onto hers with a predatory intensity.

Her jaw tightened as she focused again. The air around her shimmered as she called forth another spell. But this time, she forced herself to breathe and steady her trembling hands. She envisioned what she needed: something strong enough to bind him, to hold him down.

A rope. No. A dozen ropes.

Elle dragged her arms back, then, with every ounce of strength and precision, she flung them forward.

The magic responded instantly.

Strands of glowing energy shot forth from Elle's outstretched palms like serpents unleashed from their lair. They twisted and coiled before converging on their target- Surtr's massive torso. The glowing ropes wrapped around him. First his arms, pinning them to his sides, then his chest, and his legs, until he was entangled in their luminous grip.

Surtr roared as he struggled against the magical bindings. His movements violent but futile. Each attempt to break free only tightened the ropes further. He stumbled under their weight before collapsing onto the cold floor with a crash.

Thadren staggered back, wide-eyed as he stared at Surtr's restrained form. He turned to Elle. "How did you-"

Sweat trickled down her temple as she fought to keep the ropes intact. Her legs trembled, threatening to give out at any moment.

Surtr glared up at her from where he lay bound on the floor, his molten eyes still burning with hatred, but something else too. A flicker of respect... or perhaps fear? He bared his teeth in a grimace that might have been a smile if it weren't so filled with malice.

"You think this will hold me forever?" he sneered, his deep voice laced with venom and defiance.

"They may not burn you, but they cannot be broken." Elle wasn't certain that was true, but she prayed it was.

"Let me out of these, or I'll kill you," Surtr yelled.

Elle closed her hand and turned her wrist. The ropes tightened against Surtr, and he struggled to breathe.

Without warning, Tanngnjóstr reared back and head-butted Surtr, sending him flying into the stone wall. Surtr crumpled, and Tanngrisnir kicked him in the stomach.

Surtr groaned and rolled on his back. "I'll eat both of you and break all your bones, so you can't come back," he roared.

The dangerous-looking woman pushed the giant goats aside with ease.

"All right, you giant walking sweaters, I can handle things from here." She stopped, directly over Surtr, and lowered her trident to his chest.

He flexed against the ropes, and one of them snapped. "I will kill you, daughter."

Hel pressed her trident into his chest as another rope snapped.

Surtr yelled out, and Elle threw more fiery ropes at him. The new ropes sprouted clawed hooks at the ends, which bit into Surtr's skin, drawing blood.

"Don't worry," said the woman. "I got this." She turned to Surtr. "Surtr, king of the fire giants. Murderer of Asgardians. I, Hel, daughter of Loki and Goddess of Death, do hereby commit you to the depths of Helheim, as a prisoner. Never again to hurt anyone."

Before Surtr protested, Hel pressed the trident into his chest. It passed through him and hit the floor below. Surtr screamed in agony as the black smoke encircled him. It started at his chest and swirled outward until he was cocooned. Elle's ropes disappeared under their inky depths.

A giant pit opened in the floor, and he dropped through.

Long after her father disappeared, Elle still made out the curses he spewed at her and Hel about how he would kill them.

Hel lifted her trident, and the floor stones rolled back into place. The black smoke sucked into Hel's trident and snaked up her arm before disappearing into her dress.

That was unsettling.

Hel turned to Thor. "I believe that concludes my reason for being here, yes?"

Thor inclined his head. "Thank you, cousin."

Hel smiled. "No. Thank you. I haven't had this much fun since... forever. And now I go to make sure Surtr is completely uncomfortable in his new abode." She winked at Elle. "Be sure to come visit me when you have time. I'd love to pick your brain about the best ways to torture him." Hel backed through a shadowy portal and disappeared before Elle answered.

No one moved for several seconds as they stared at the spot where Surtr had lain.

Thor rushed to Elle. "Are you all right?"

She nodded.

He inspected her, and the lighting in his eyes vanished. "I'm sorry. I'm so sorry."

"No," she said. "I am sorry. I should have told you."

He shook his head and kissed her. "It doesn't matter. I don't care who your father was, I only care who you are."

"And who am I?" she asked.

"The woman I love and whom I hope will consent to marrying a lowly mechanic who lives in Helheim fixing bikes and trying to be worthy of you for the rest of my existence."

Elle's body exploded with warmth as she encircled Thor's neck with her arms. "I wouldn't dream of being anyone else."

Thor pulled her closer, his lips finding hers in an electrifying kiss that sent shivers racing down her spine like tiny currents of lightning. The world seemed to fall away. She lost all sense of time as he kissed her over and over, his strong hands crushing her against him.

"Is that it?" Baldur finally asked.

"No fighting?" Vidarr moaned.

"Man, I got all dressed up and have nowhere to go," said Hermódr. "This armor isn't easy to put on."

"Perhaps the new fire giant king will allow us to spar with some of his men, so it isn't a total waste," said Hödr.

Elle chuckled and broke her kiss with Thor.

The group looked at Thadren.

"Of course," said Thadren. "Anything we can do to heal relations with the Asgardians."

Elle smiled. She made the right decision with Thadren.

"Can we kill them?" Fenrir growled.

"No!" everyone said together.

"You lot have gone soft." Fenrir stalked to the door and raced out.

Tanngrisnir and Tanngnjóstr bleated at Elle and pressed their heads into her.

She chuckled and scratched their noses. "All right. Who are my great big protectors? Did you save me? Yes, you did. Yes, you did."

"They saved you?" Thor questioned.

She turned and winked at him. "You all saved me."

Thor looked at the goats, then at her. "You know they are going to be unbearable to live with now, thinking they are the heroes."

She smiled and kissed him. "I'm pretty sure all three of you will."

CHAPTER FIFTEEN

Soaring across the cosmos, Thor held onto the chariot with one arm and wrapped his other around Elle, who clung to him so tight he could barely breathe. A joy unlike anything he'd ever known surged within him. Tanngrisnir and Tanngnjóstr streaked through the heavens like twin comets, their coats glimmering under the nebula's glow.

The rush of cold wind whistled in his ears as they descended beneath the old constellations. Clusters of distant planets blurred past them. The brisk atmosphere carried a sharp scent reminiscent of clean frost mingling with electric ozone. As they sped toward Helheim's ethereal gateway shimmering on the horizon, Thor couldn't believe the turn his life had taken in a short span of a week.

They headed for the portal, and before they entered, Val flew by, followed by Loki.

"Really?" Thor called. "You couldn't wait your turn."

Val looked back. "This is my turn."

Elle snickered, and they dove through the portal.

"That one is a pistol," said Thor.

Elle smiled. "You have no idea."

"I'm glad she is. Loki deserves a woman he can't handle after everything he's done."

"Yes," Elle replied. "But does Val deserve him after everything she's been through?"

Thor thought for a moment and wondered if Val had suffered the same abuse Elle had. As a prisoner of Surtr's, he assumed she had, but somehow he doubted she would take a beating from anyone without putting up a fight. Even at the cost of her life.

The chariot popped through the portal, and the Helborn guard on duty dove to the ground as they rushed by. He jumped back to his feet despite wearing full armor and swore at Thor.

Thor waved and continued on.

"I think we scared him," said Elle.

"More likely, we woke him from his nap."

Tanngrisnir and Tanngnjóstr clopped down the street, and as they neared the shop, they shrank to the size of bison, then to the size of horses, and finally to their more manageable sizes. They stopped outside the shop's back door.

"It's been a long time since we've been out for a race across the stars, hasn't it, boys?" Thor scratched their backs, and the goats bleated and pawed at the ground.

Thor helped Elle from the chariot and hoisted the heavy chest full of her belongings off as well. He carried the chest to the door and returned to unharness the goats.

"I quite enjoyed the ride," said Elle. "Perhaps we can make it a regular thing."

Thor stared at her. "You jest?"

She shook her head. "No. It was quite thrilling. And if

Tanngrisnir and Tanngnjóstr like it, why not? Mortals take their dogs for a walk; why can't we take the goats for a run?"

Thor's heart swelled. He couldn't love her more. He'd never taken a woman on his chariot before, but with Elle, like everything else with her, it felt right.

"If you think that is thrilling, wait until you experience the rush of the wind on your face as we ride down the coast on my bike."

Elle nodded. "Sorry, but I'm sure nothing will compare to being pulled across the nine realms by two enormous thundering goats."

She was probably right.

Thor opened the door and hefted her out of the way. The goats butted in and ran straight for their water trough.

"Manners!" Thor called before taking Elle's hand. "You'd think they were raised by animals or something."

Elle laughed. "Teaching them some manners will be quite an adventure for the future."

The future. He hardly believed he was talking about it with someone.

Thor led her out to the shop floor and picked her up, carrying her up the winding metal staircase to his apartment above. He pushed the door inward, and Elle stared, wide-eyed as she took in his place.

"What the..."

Thor chuckled and walked through the entrance to the living room and set her on the plush white rug.

"Where did you find all this?"

Thor looked around the cream-and-green interior of his apartment. He'd spent close to a hundred years procuring the items for every inch of his place. Sculptures from Norway. Tables and artifacts from the Netherlands. An authentic four-poster cherry wood sleigh bed, complete with posters carved as dragons, from Sweden. Every single item in his apartment had been purchased from a private collector or a museum. As far as Thor was concerned, he'd made his apartment as close to Asgard as possible. He walked to the massive hutch on one wall and began taking off his armor, placing it back where it had sat before that day, untouched for centuries.

He unstrapped his breastplate and slung it over his head. "Mainly Europe. Though not from Asgard, it's all Norse, and I was able to rebuild or repair everything in poor condition. Everything except the kitchen, of course, that's state of the art."

Elle walked into the kitchen and ran her fingers over the granite countertop. "You do remember that I can't cook, right?"

He unstrapped his shin guards. "It still looks nice. And if you ever want to learn, you'll have the best money can buy."

She raised her eyebrows and smirked like there was a joke he wasn't in on.

She stepped into the dining room, and Thor removed his boots and followed her in.

She stared at the table shaped like a Viking long boat. The sixty-foot boat had taken a lot of finessing to fit into his apartment, but it had been worth it.

"It's called an Oseberg ship," said Thor. "It was discovered in a burial mound in Norway. I had to resurface the wood. I think I did a decent job."

Elle stared at the glass-covered boat. "This is... amazing," she said. "How many people does it fit?"

"Thirty, on each side, probably. I've never had anyone over to use it, so I'm not sure."

Elle walked along the table, running her fingers over the backs of the chairs. "A real Viking ship. With dragon's heads carved in the front and back. Incredible." Her gaze traveled over the intricate scrollwork, and Thor felt a sense of pride at her admiration.

She chuckled. "I think you underestimate how many people would fit at this table."

"When we host our first family dinner, we can find out."

Elle's gaze shot to his. "We?" She stopped moving. "You still want there to be a 'we'?"

In the rush of everything that had happened, Thor hadn't had time to think about what they had been through. The lying, but also the honesty. The tears, but also the laughter. The fear, but also the immense happiness.

"I do," he said. "I don't like that you didn't tell me about your past, but... I did tell you it didn't matter to me who you were, only who you are. And unless I lied to you, I have to be okay with you not telling me."

She nodded and continued down the table.

Thor's gut clenched. Had she changed her mind? Had her newfound independence caused her to see he wasn't worthy of her?

"What about you?" he asked. "You aren't obligated to me because my family came to your rescue."

She stopped, and her eyes narrowed. "You are aware I could've handled myself. I was doing fine before you showed up."

Thor wrinkled up his face. "Were you, though?"

Elle threw her hands in front of her, and a group of thick, fiery bands flew from her fingers and snaked around his body. The ropes warmed but did not burn his skin.

"I can heat them up for you if they aren't warm enough," she chided.

Arousal stirred inside Thor. He flexed against the bands, but they didn't budge. He flexed again, this time trying to break free. Elle raised her palm, and the bands tightened around him.

She smirked.

A thrill of excitement mixed with a trickle of fear inside him. He'd never been bound by something he couldn't break.

Elle sauntered around the table toward him.

"Have you been able to do this all along?"

"Among other things. I told you I literally made the jewelry with my hands."

"I see that now." He tested the bands again.

They didn't budge.

Elle stopped a foot from him and looked him up and down. For the first time, he took a long look at her in her curve-hugging dress. The sight made his arousal kick up. How had he *not* noticed before? Maybe it was because he'd been focused on making sure she wasn't married off to someone else.

Elle glided towards him, pulling a wooden chair from the table with an easy grace. Smoothly placing it behind him, she gave a gentle push until he settled into its embrace. Her eyes twinkled with mischief as she circled around, laying her fingers on the ethereal bands. They shimmered and writhed like serpents, sliding off his chest to tightly coil around his arms, securing him to the chair. With a playful smile, she perched herself on his lap.

Thor strained against the magical bindings; every fiber of his being screamed to hold her close. The intensity of his desire was a tempest, threatening to burst forth at any moment.

Elle's features glowed. A mesmerizing mixture of light and darkness woven together under her skin like an enchanted tapestry.

Elle leaned closer, and warmth radiated from her body like

basking in sunlight after days beneath stormy skies. His heart thundered, matching the wild chaos of emotions swirling between them.

An unspoken electricity flowed between them; a promise hanging heavy amidst whispered desires.

He flexed again, wanting to grab onto her. To hold her.

Elle gripped his chin. "Don't break the chair. I like it."

Thor fought to control himself as Elle's hands moved up his chest, her fingers threading through his hair. The sensation made him groan.

Elle leaned in with purpose, catching his bottom lip between her teeth before teasing him with a slow slip of her tongue. Thor responded, kissing her with an intensity that belied his restraint, only for her to pull back.

"I'm in charge now." Her voice came out confident, carrying the weight of newfound authority.

Thor couldn't suppress a grin. "Wow. So you've found your big girl voice."

"You've taught me many things, Thor Odinson," she replied with a smirk playing on her lips. "It's time I show you the creature you've unleashed, and what it's like when a woman holds the reins."

His entire body tensed, each muscle coiled like steel wire beneath his skin. As he sat hoping not to break the chair under him, he realized how eager he was for what might come next under her command. It stirred both curiosity and apprehension in equal measure.

“Have you ever let a woman be in control before?” She backed up before undoing the buttons down the side of her dress.

“No,” he admitted, his erection groaning against his leather pants.

She slid the dress from her body agonizingly slowly, spending seconds revealing a mere inch.

Thor's mouth dried. His fingers curled into fists as the golden fabric slid down over her breasts, revealing the white, silky fabric underneath. She moved with deliberate slowness, her hazel eyes never leaving his face as she watched his reaction.

The dress pooled at her feet, and she stepped out of it, standing before him in nothing but the delicate undergarments. The sight of her, confident, powerful, commanding, sent a jolt through him that had nothing to do with his godhood and everything to do with the woman he'd encouraged her to unleash.

Elle walked around behind him, her fingers trailing across his shoulders. Her breath fell against his ear as she leaned close.

"Do you know what it's like," she whispered, "to spend your entire life being told what to do? When to speak, when to be silent, where to stand, how to move?" Her hands slid down his chest, nails dragging through his shirt. "Always at someone else's mercy."

Thor's breathing quickened. He finally understood. She wasn't just seducing him, but claiming the power that had been stolen from her for so long.

"You're right," he managed, his voice rough. "I did create this. And I wouldn't change a damn thing."

She came around to face him, standing between his spread legs. She flicked her fingers at the fireplace in the corner, and it caught with a small explosion. She flicked another fiery red rope toward the door, and the lights overhead extinguished.

The firelight from the hearth cast dancing shadows across her skin, making her look otherworldly. The delicate white satin did little to hide her form, and Thor had to remind himself to breathe.

"Good answer." She traced a finger along his jaw, then down his throat. "Because I'm not done with you yet."

Elle straddled him again, settling herself against him. Thunder sounded outside, and she smiled. The heat of her core pressed against his erection through his pants, and he flexed hard against the magical bands, making the chair creak.

"Easy," she murmured, rolling her hips. "I told you not to break it."

"Then stop torturing me."

"You think this is torture?" Her eyebrows arched. "Thor Odinson, I haven't even begun."

She kissed him again, deeper this time, her tongue sliding against his as her hands worked at the buttons of his shirt. She worked them free one by one, her fingers brushing against his chest with each movement. The contact sent electricity skittering across his skin. When she finally pushed the shirt open, her palms flattened against his bare chest, and she traced the scars with curious fingertips.

"Tell me about this one," she said, touching a jagged mark that ran from his collarbone to his sternum.

"Ice giant. About fifteen hundred years ago."

She leaned down and pressed her lips to the scar, and Thor's head fell back. The sensation of her mouth on his skin while he couldn't touch her was exquisite agony.

"And this one?" She moved to another scar on his ribs.

"Troll. Norway. Can't remember when."

Another kiss. Another jolt of pleasure. She was mapping him, learning him, claiming every part of him that battle had marked. The bands around his arms tightened as he strained against them, desperate to pull her closer.

"Elle," he groaned. "Please."

"Please, what?" She looked up at him through her thick lashes, and the firelight caught in her eyes, making them glow amber and golden.

"Please," he said, his voice rougher than he'd intended. "Touch me."

She smiled. "I am touching you."

She slid off his lap, and the loss of her warmth made him want to roar in frustration, but then she knelt before him, her hands working at his belt.

Thor's breath caught. The sight of her between his legs, completely in control, was almost more than he could handle. The leather of his pants strained against him as she pulled the belt free and tossed it aside.

"You know," she said as if discussing the weather and not engaged in something driving him insane, "Val always told me that men were simple creatures. That they wanted one thing and once they had it, they moved on."

Her fingers traced the line of his waistband, and Thor had to concentrate to form words. "Val doesn't know everything."

"Doesn't she?" Elle looked up at him, and something vulnerable flickered across her face before the mask of confidence returned. "Then tell me what you want, Thor. What do you really want from me?"

The question hung between them, weighted with more than that moment. Thor understood she wasn't asking about sex. She was asking about everything. Their future, his intentions, whether he would still want her when the novelty wore off, when she wasn't new and exciting anymore.

"I want everything," he said, his voice steady despite the fire raging through him. "I want to wake up next to you every morning. I want to teach you to ride my motorcycle and take you to every restaurant in Los Angeles until we find your favorite. I want to argue with you about raw fish and watch you play with the goats. I want to help you discover who you are when no one is controlling you."

Her eyes glistened in the firelight.

"I want to watch you grow into the powerful woman you're meant to be," he continued. "I want to be there when you decide what you want to do with your life. I want to hold you when the nightmares come, and I want you to hold me when mine do. I want to build a life with you, Elle. Not just tonight. Every night. For as long as you'll have me."

A tear slipped down her cheek, and she brushed it away. "You're sure?"

"More sure than I've ever been." She studied his face for a long moment, searching for any hint of deception, any crack in his sincerity. Thor held her gaze, letting her see everything. The vulnerability, the hope, the absolute certainty that had taken root in his chest the moment he'd realized she was gone.

"Then you should know something." Her fingers stilled on his waistband. "I don't know how to be what you need. I don't know how to be a partner or a lover or- or whatever this is supposed to be. All I know is how to survive. How to be small and quiet and invisible."

"That's not all you know." Thor leaned forward as much as the bands would allow. "You know how to be brave. You stood up to Surtr. You claimed your power. You chose your own path."

"Because you showed me."

"No." He shook his head. "I didn't show you anything. It was always there, Elle. I just gave you a safe place to let it out."

She bit her lip. The firelight painted her skin in shades of gold and orange. She flicked her wrist, and the bands disappeared. He lurched forward and captured her mouth with his.

Picking her up, he wrapped her legs around his waist and carried her toward his bedroom, lit only by the ambient glow filtering in from the living room fireplace. He laid Elle on the massive dragon-carved bed, the mattress giving under their combined weight. The posts rose toward the ceiling like ancient sentinels, and for a moment, he was transported- not to Asgard, but to something better. Something entirely his own.

Elle's hair spread across his pillow in waves of auburn and ginger, and the sight made his chest constrict. She belonged there. In his bed, in his life, in every moment going forward.

He braced himself above her, drinking in the sight of her flushed cheeks and swollen lips. Her chest rose and fell with quick breaths, and heat radiated from her skin even through the thin satin.

"You're staring," she whispered.

"I'm memorizing." He traced the curve of her cheek with his thumb. "Every time I look at you, I find something new."

“What have you found so far?” she asked.

"That you're impossibly beautiful," he murmured, lowering his head to kiss along her collarbone. "That you have a small scar right next to your earlobe." His lips moved lower, tracing the edge of the satin. "That your skin is a constellation of freckles I want to count." He kissed her abdomen. “That your belly button dips in, but at the bottom it pokes out a little too.”

Elle's fingers threaded through his hair, and the gentle tug sent pleasure spiraling down his spine. He worked his way across her skin, savoring each gasp and sigh that escaped her lips.

"Thor..." Her voice wavered.

He lifted his head. "What is it?"

He waited, giving her the space to find her words. Emotions flickered across her face. Desire, uncertainty, something deeper that made his heart clench.

"I'm afraid," she whispered.

"Of me?"

"Of losing this. Of waking up and finding it was all a dream." Her wide, round eyes searched his face. "Of you realizing I'm not worth all this trouble."

Thor cupped her face, forcing her to look at him. "Listen to me. You are worth everything. Every breath. Every lonely moment of my existence. Ragnarök itself. All of it, I would do a thousand times again if it meant I got to have you now and forever."

Elle yanked him to her, her lips claiming his mouth. He kissed her back with fervor. She wrapped her legs around his waist and flipped him on his back. They stripped off the remainder of their clothes, and before he gained his bearings, she pushed him back on the pillows and slid down on him. He grabbed her hips as her silken body wrapped around him.

He swore in Olde Norse and grabbed her hips. She stared into his eyes as she rocked her hips on his. Thor stared at her. Beautiful, radiant, and his.

Her rhythm picked up, and his orgasm pulsed up the back of his legs. His erection throbbed and tightened, wanting release.

Not yet. Not until she got hers.

He moved his fingers between them, finding the sensitive spot that made her gasp. She gripped his shoulders as their bodies moved together.

Suddenly, she sucked in a breath, and her eyes went completely golden. She stared straight at him as every inch of her burned bright and warm. The sensation sent him over the edge as she cried his name. Rocking her hips against him harder. His body spasmed as it spilled into her. He pulled her through her climax as she called to him over and over.

Lightning lit up the sky outside as thunder crashed against the walls, making them shake.

Finally, she fell on his chest.

"That… was… amazing," she breathed.

"Midgard-shattering?"

"Helheim ending."

He kissed her soft, making her mewl into his mouth.

"I love you, Thor Odinson."

He brushed her cheek. "And I love you, Sutrelle, daughter of Aelena, of Asgard."

EPILOGUE

It'd been three months since Thor and Elle had met, and they still couldn't go a day without putting their hands all over each other. She was glad their bed was right above Thor's shop; it made it convenient… though they'd broken in almost every surface of his property. Including one of his bikes.

He'd helped convince Elle to start making jewelry, so they'd turned the backroom from a sparring room into a shop for her to work in. She hardly believed she owned her own business. She'd named it *If the Ring Fits*, proud of her own cleverness. Thor had taken her down to the jewelry district of Los Angeles, where she had sold her largest ruby to purchase many smaller uncut stones and gold to make her creations. And to her surprise, though she hadn't been open that long, and she hadn't finished many pieces to stock the shop, she'd had dozens of custom orders come in from Thor's family.

At first, she'd thought they were being kind, but then she'd started getting orders from patrons and employees of both the Raven Weaver and Valhalla's Throne.

She finished setting a pink sapphire into a platinum setting when her loud rock music shut off.

Tanngrisnir and Tanngnjóstr complained from their pen, and Elle turned from her workbench to find Thor walking toward her.

"Time to get ready."

She set the ring in a velvet box to finish later. "The food needs to go in the warmer."

"Done."

"Did you turn it on?"

"Like you showed me."

"What about the cake? Did you take it from the fridge so I can frost it?"

"Sitting on the counter next to your frosting and cake knives."

"And the wine-"

"Chilled and ready to go. The only thing you need to do is whatever you need to."

Elle went through her list in her mind to make sure she was ready to host her first family dinner.

"Do you think I made enough meat?" she asked.

Thor wrapped his arms around her and kissed her cheek. "Elle. You have been taking cooking lessons with my father for two months. You took baking lessons from Melli for three months. All to make this one meal. You had the table set a week ago. Everything is ready. And remember, it's our family. It doesn't have to be perfect."

"But I want it to be perfect. It's the first time I've hosted a family dinner."

"And that's why no matter what you do, everyone will love it.

Because they love you, and they want you to be happy. Except for maybe Fenrir, he doesn't care what anyone thinks about anything."

Thor kissed her head and swatted her on the rear. "Go put on that sexy new dress my mother made."

Her heart pattered thinking about the dress. "It really is beautiful."

"It should be, it's like your jewelry, one of a kind. Now go, before I have to come up and help you shower." He winked at her.

"If you did that, dinner would be late."

"We could always reschedule for tomorrow."

She pushed away from him. "No. I've done too much work."

"Then you'd better hurry, they'll be here in thirty minutes."

"Thirty? I told you to tell me when I had an hour left." She rushed toward the door.

"I did," he called. "But you couldn't hear me over the music."

Elle shook her head and jogged to the winding metal stairs. She had to hurry.

DINNER AROUND THE OSEBERG SHIP TABLE HAD GONE MORE beautifully than Elle imagined. There had been enough food for everyone, and they'd all praised her new cooking skills. As she brought out the delicate three-tier cake for everyone to enjoy, Thor got to his feet and tapped a fork against his wine glass.

A hush fell over the group.

"Thank you all for coming to our first family dinner. And a special thank you to Elle for all her hard work, not just in putting this together for us, but for putting up with us as well."

Several chuckles sounded around the table.

"And as Elle has now spent months putting up with me, I think

I've convinced her to stick around." Thor set down his glass and walked to Elle.

He touched her cheek, and every inch of Elle's body warmed. He kissed her and lowered to one knee.

Elle's skin flushed.

He pulled a black velvet box from his pocket and held it out to her.

Elle's heart beat so fast she was sure she would pass out. Around the table, everyone from Odin and Frigg to Val and Heimdall smiled at her. The intimidating faces of Tyr, and Hel smiled in their own way. Even Fenrir appeared less hostile than normal.

Elle opened the box, and inside sat an intricately woven band of Celtic knots entwined with hearts. And at the center of each heart sat a brilliant red ruby.

Elle's chest squeezed.

"The work isn't as refined as what you are able to do, but I did make it myself. Of course, Tanngrisnir and Tanngnjóstr helped pick the stones from your stash."

Elle sniffled as tears flooded her eyes.

"I can buy you a different one if you don't-"

"I love it," she blurted.

"Is that a yes?"

"You still have time to say no and choose me," said Baldur.

"Sorry, Baldur," said Elle. "I chose Thor the first time I saw him."

Thor stood and pulled her into a hug, kissing her so passionately that it felt like the first time.

Everyone broke into cheers and clapped.

Odin stood as Thor put the ring on her finger.

"Congrats to Thor Odinson and Princess Sutrelle, daughter of Aelena, Priestess of Asgard."

Everyone raised their wine glasses. Thor kissed her again, and Elle grew so warm she was sure her hair would catch fire.

Loki and Val approached them. "Congratulations, cousin." Loki hugged Thor.

Val smiled in a way Elle hadn't seen her before. She kissed Elle's cheek. "I'm happy for you."

Elle squeezed Val's hand.

"Now," said Thor. "When are you two going to make it official?"

Val rolled her eyes. "When Hel lets Surtr out of prison."

Everyone burst into laughter.

"Would you like to make a wager?" asked Loki.

Val eyed him. "Why not?"

Loki's grin spread across his face. "Because I always win a bet."

Val threw him a brilliant smile. "Then losing will be a new experience for you."

Thor barked with laughter. "Oh, Cousin, you are in so much trouble with this one, and I can't tell you just how much I absolutely love that."

LOKI'S WARRIOR MATE

GODS AND MONSTERS FATED MATES

Rebekah R. Ganiere

CHAPTER ONE

"I can't believe I let you talk me into this."

Loki rolled his eyes. "I think it's your mother you have to thank. I simply asked if you would go with me because I have someone I need to meet, and I don't want to get roped into conversations with other Sups looking for free legal advice."

Thor threw him a daggered gaze. "You mean a meeting you happened to mention in my mother's presence, which happened to be on the same night as her monthly masquerade feast?"

Loki chuckled and straightened his shirt cuffs. "Wrong again, my boy. Your mother set up the meeting. It's not my fault you're so nosy you eavesdropped on the conversation and got tangled up in her little scheme to marry you off."

He wasn't about to tell Thor that the conversation he'd had with Frigg had been prearranged to try to lure Thor into going to the masquerade. The morning before the conversation, Loki had been awakened by his cellphone. He hadn't needed to look at it to know it was Frigg.

He'd had a dream involving Thor, a woman, and the masquerade. And if he'd had a dream about Thor meeting a woman, there was absolutely no doubt Frigg had as well. So, he'd answered his phone and set up a time and place for the meeting where Frigg knew Thor would be. And here they were, one week later, Loki playing babysitter and making sure Thor went to the party just like he was supposed to.

Loki delved into Thor's thoughts for a moment and then set his hand on Thor's shoulder. "It won't be any different if you don't give it a chance."

Thor shrugged off Loki's touch. "I hate it when you do that. Reading minds is creepy."

Loki shrugged. "I wouldn't need to if you opened your mouth and spoke more. You used to be so talkative. Couldn't stop talking as I remember. Mostly about yourself. Your conquests, victories, virtues, anything about you. But now-"

"Now I know better." Thor grabbed his leather coat and threw it on.

Loki checked his hair in the mirror. "I was going to say, now you're boring."

"And what about you?" Thor questioned. "I don't see you rushing out to find someone."

A permanent relationship was the last thing Loki was looking for. He'd been married. And he'd had kids. Now he was content to sample all that the Nine Realms had to offer.

Loki flashed him a winning smile. "I don't need to. My bed is constantly filled with whomever I find companionable for the night. No strings. No expectations. Just fun. The way I like it."

Thor walked to the edge of his loft and took the stairs down to his shop floor, two at a time. Bikes lined the walls of the solid brick structure.

"No time for fiddling with that," said Loki. "I still don't know why you mess with those things when you can fly."

"What about you and your squashed, brightly colored cars? You can fly, why do you drive those things?"

"Touché." Loki inclined his head.

"Besides," said Thor. "I like taking them apart and rebuilding them the way I want them. Gives me something to focus on."

Thor headed over and picked up Mjölnir.

"My car is out front." Loki pulled his key fob from his pocket and headed to the exit.

"I can make my own way there." Thor lifted his hammer to the sky and, as always, disappeared in a flash of light.

Loki shook his head. What was the fun of being in Helheim if you were just going to stick to doing things the way you always had?

Loki exited the building and smiled at his metallic lime green Lamborghini. He owned over a dozen cars, but the Lambo was for sure his favorite. And when he took it down to the demon street races, he couldn't help but win. Which was exactly what he intended on doing right after he got Frigg's most recent refugees their papers.

VAL SCANNED THE BEAUTIFUL, EXPANSIVE GROUNDS OF THE MANSION, where people milled about.

"Are you sure this is where Lady Frigg said we were to meet Loki?" Elle asked.

Yup. Val glanced through the gold gates, then at the paper in her hand again, before showing it to Elle.

Lady Frigg's mansion was all the paper said, and it was pretty hard to miss her mansion in Helheim. Especially the giant ornate metal gates. This was definitely Frigg's place.

Val sighed. *So unnecessary.* What was Loki up to? Or Frigg, for that matter? A party? Really?

"Come on," said Val. "Let's get this over with, and then we can go back to Midgard."

Elle nodded. Val led her across the green and past a marble fountain to the colored-glass front doors. Greenery and vines snaked up the front of the building. Standing near the entrance, a wide-shouldered, cobalt blue-skinned male nodded at people as they entered.

Val assessed him as they approached and flexed her wrists, making sure her wrist blades still worked. Not that they wouldn't. She always needed to check though, just in case…

She strode up the cream marble steps toward the entrance. Suddenly, the scent morphed into something spicy and warm. Cinnamon mixed with cognac. It made her relax a fraction as she breathed it in, before she tensed and growled.

Great. Frigg was putting something in the air to make people relax. Well, to hel with that. That was not happening. Not for her. Not here.

Though they'd been out of Surtr's realm for a month, Val had yet to let her guard down. Armed from the shoulders downward, she didn't allow herself to slack off for even a moment. She spent close to 3 hours every night continuing her training before bed. And the first thing she did when she awoke each day was to walk to Sutrelle's apartment door and make sure the princess was safe.

"Stay close," said Val

A young woman with long golden braids and bright eyes glided over to them and smiled. "Hello. I'm Fulla. You must be new here."

Val recognized Frigg's handmaiden immediately. Just how many Asgardians were in Helheim?

"I'm Val. We have a meeting-"

Fulla smiled brighter. "Of course. Lady Frigg said you would be coming." She looked at Elle. "You must be Elle."

The hairs raised on Val's neck. Something was definitely off about this meeting. Val's eyebrows smashed together. "I don't understand. We were told to be here at 8:00."

Fulla nodded. "If you will just put these on and follow me, I can get you ladies a table."

Val looked from Elle to Fulla. Being in Helheim made Val twitchy. There were too many prying eyes. Too many loose lips. And too many oversized ears itching for any piece of gossip that could get them a leg up.

Val opened her mouth to decline, but Elle stepped forward.

"Thank you, Fulla." Elle took the masks and handed Val the silver fox mask while she herself affixed a golden cat mask to her face. Elle grabbed Val's hand and followed Fulla toward the tables lining a red velvet curtain.

"This is strange," said Val. "Why do we need masks to get a table to talk to Loki?"

"Maybe it's a game? Or maybe it's to protect our identities? He has a lot of clients. I'm sure we aren't the only ones he is helping. Maybe he is trying to help us not be recognized. I'll get us some food, and you have a drink." Elle threw Val a smile.

Val wanted to object, but as she looked around, she realized that if she played along, they were less likely to be recognized in the sea of masked faces.

Slowly, she walked to a table strategically set so that she could keep an eye on the ballroom.

Val's back itched between her shoulder blades, and she fought against scratching. She knew what the itch meant, and it'd been getting worse and worse lately, particularly when in Helheim.

Val glanced over to where Elle stood picking out a plate of food from the long table.

Sutrelle's body language relaxed as she perused the delicacies. But the instant she relaxed, Val became even more alert. Because the moment Sutrelle began to relax was the moment Val needed to be more vigilant than ever. Sutrelle knew that running from her father could mean her death if she was caught, but Val had experienced exactly what Surtr did to those he deemed a traitor – and death was the very last thing Surtr would have in mind for them if he caught them.

A moment passed, and Val looked around for a bar, but it was all the way on the other side of the room. Damn,

The growing crowd of people made her twitchy. She wanted to get the documents she needed and get Sutrelle back to their apartments above Frigg's bar.

Ever since they'd run from Muspelheim, Val had been more on edge than ever. But Lady Frigg had taken them in and offered them shelter, and Loki finally had the human paperwork needed to permanently change their identities, bringing them one step closer to freedom. It irritated Val how many different pieces of identification humans needed to live on Midgard. Birth certificate, Social Security Number, Real ID? It was as if Midgard was afraid they'd lose people, or worse, they wanted to keep tabs on their every movement. Much like Surtr had.

Living on Midgard the last month had been… strange. The sights, smells, and noise of Los Angeles were nothing like what she was used to. And the people, especially the men, left something to be desired. On dozens of occasions, she had been hit on, flirted with, and flat-out objectified by the human men. And in every instance, she had made each of them a bet. If they could beat her in an arm-wrestling contest, she would have a drink with them. But if they lost, they would have to give her the money they would have spent on the two drinks instead. So far, she'd won over a thousand Midgardian dollars.

A hand jutted in front of Val's face, holding a flute of champagne. She tensed and looked up.

A tall, crimson-skinned man with broad horns like a minotaur wearing a golden elephant mask smiled at her, revealing bright, sharp teeth.

Val stared at the champagne but didn't take it. "New would infer that I had any desire to be here right now, which I don't. So, no, I'm not new here, I'm just stopping by to pick something up."

His head cocked to the side, and he chuckled. "Okay."

She got the distinct idea that he had no idea what she'd even said. "Is this your first time here?"

He shook his heavy head. "Nope. Been coming for more years than I can count. Just hoping tonight will finally be the night."

"The night for what?" she asked.

He smiled again. "For me to finally find the one I am meant to be with."

And that was her cue. "Well, I hope you find her. Or him. Or… whomever."

The male continued to stand there for several seconds, hand still outstretched, but when she didn't move, he finally walked away.

What the hel was that? Were they at a mating party?

"Hello, Val." Lady Frigg smiled and handed Val a mug of something heady. "Thank you for coming."

Val swigged the drink, the sweet taste gliding across her tongue, but making her teeth ache.

"Was this your doing or his?" Val set the mug on the table.

Frigg continued to smile. "I just thought this would be a good place to meet since you could be in disguise and there would be food and drink, and I thought it might be easier for you to relax in such an atmosphere."

Val studied Frigg. She was beautiful and genuine, but also held the mischievousness of a mother trying to get what she wanted for her family.

"So is he going to show up or…"

Frigg chuckled. "Loki always likes to make an entrance. He should be here any minute."

Val snorted. "Yeah... He's always been an attention whore."

Frigg cocked her head. "You know him?"

She knew him all right. She knew all about him from her Valkyrie sisters, who had all taken a tumble or two in his bed. She would call him a manwhore- but there were more Norse gods who had bedded as many women as Loki than there were those who hadn't. So, how could she possibly judge? Just because she'd never given it up to the god of mischief didn't mean she was a saint.

"I've seen him. And let's say I had a lot of sisters who... spent time with him. His reputation precedes him even larger than his ego."

Frigg burst into a tinkle of laughter so contagious that Val almost smiled herself.

Frigg winked at Val and squeezed her shoulder. “I’m so glad you came. You really are quite perfect.”

Before Val could ask her what she meant, Frigg swept away and headed toward another table.

Val tracked Sutrelle as she made her way to a table and sat.

Sigh… she had no idea what Frigg had gotten them into, but so far, she didn’t like it.

As Loki walked up the steps of Frigg’s mansion, several of the females waved to greet him. Loki smiled politely and continued on through the door. Thor walked to Loki and shoved a mask into his chest.

"What's this?" Loki inspected the mask and scowled. "You didn't."

"If I have to, you have to."

Loki scowled. "Why? Frigg's not my mother. I didn't promise her anything."

"Payback."

"For what?" Thor opened his mouth, but Loki held up his hand. "Never mind. Fine. But I'm only doing this because if I don't, Frigg will have my balls for earrings. But don't think this is the end, cousin."

Thor snorted, and Loki knew what he was thinking. They may both be Norse Gods, but they were far from being any kind of blood relation. The closest relation to Loki besides his children was Thor's adoptive mother, Frigg.

Loki sighed before affixing the lion mask to his face and looking around the tables for the person he'd come to meet. Long blonde hair and a straight ramrod spine caught his gaze. She sat at a table, both perfectly positioned for defense as well as making a swift exit if necessary. It was the exact table he would have chosen, so it had to be her. A shiver skittered over his skin, making him want to turn around and run out the door.

"Don't tell me you're scared," asked a sultry voice.

Loki glanced at Frigg. The glint in her eyes told him she was up to something, but it didn't matter. Whatever she had up her sleeve wouldn't work. He was more than happy with his life, and he intended to keep it just the way it was.

Instead, he simply inclined his head, smiled, and strode for the table.

Dear Reader,

Thank you for taking the time to read *Thor's Fiery Mate.* I've been obsessed with mythology for as long as I can remember. The Norse Gods were always ones I wanted to write about, so I figured, why not give them their own series? I hope you enjoyed Thor and Elle's story as much as I enjoyed writing about them.

If you enjoyed the book, please take a moment to leave a review on your favorite retailer. Your reviews make all the difference to authors and to the success of books.

Feel free to take a moment to email me and let me know what you liked about the book, or who your favorite character was, and why. I love hearing from readers. It makes writing so much more fun when I hear from my readers.

VampWereZombie@Gmail.com

To find out more about me and my Upcoming Releases, Please Join my Street Team for Swag and Freebies.

I also love connecting with readers! Stalk me everywhere!

I look forward to hearing from you!

Rebekah R. Ganiere - BOOKS WITH A BITE

USA Today Bestselling Author

Rebekah R. Ganiere

Dead Awakenings

Kissed by the Reaper

Fairelle Series

Red the Were Hunter - Book One

Yanti's Choice - Free Fairelle Short Story

Snow the Vampire Slayer - Book Two

Jamen's Yuletide Bride - Book Three

Zelle and the Tower - Book Four

Cinder the Fae - Book Five

Belle and the Beast - Book Six

Gerall's Festivus Bride - Book Seven

Jak the Giant Healer - Book Eight

Olivia and the Giant - Book Nine (April 2026)

Eric's Wayward Bride - Book Ten (Coming Soon)

Wolf River

PROMISED at the Moon

CURSED by the Moon

RECLAIMED from the Moon

TAMED under the Moon

UNLEASHED with the Moon

FATED despite the Moon

FOUND because of the Moon

ROCKED (2027)

The Society Series

Reign of the Vampires

Rise of the Fae

Vengeance of the Demons

Lycan King Wars

Alpha Marked

Alpha Claimed

Alpha Queen

Alpha King (2026)

Alpha Rogue (2026)

Tharnaxian Chronicles

The First

The Many (2027)

The Last (2027)

The Otherworlder Series

Kidnapped at Christmas

Vigilante at Valentine

Massacre at Mardi Gras

Hoodwinked at Halloween

Nightmare at New Year (2026)

Gods and Monsters Fated Mates

Thor's Feiry Mate

Loki's Warrior Mate

Fenrir Innocent Mate(2026)

Tyr Celestial Mate (2026)

Freya's Eternal Mates (2027)

Nocturne Bloodlines

Queen of the Night (2026)

Protector of the Night (2026)

Son of the Night (2027)

Immortal Monsters

Dracula's Bride

Frankenstein's Bride (Coming Soon)

Happy Holiday Romances

Rekindling Christmas

Christmas Lodge

NEWSLETTER

To claim your Two FREE Books and find out more about Rebekah R. Ganiere and her other Upcoming Releases You can Go Here:
www.RebekahGaniere.com/Newsletter

www.ingramcontent.com/pod-product-compliance
Lightning Source LLC
LaVergne TN
LVHW091138080826
845145LV00008B/2191

* 9 7 8 1 6 3 3 0 0 0 9 7 1 *